FRANK

FIDGET-KNICKERS

AND THE RELUCTANT RESCUE

BY

COLIN WICKS

Illustrations by Su Wicks, and final proofs
edited by Dan McCloskey

The story and characters from this book are entirely made up from the author's imagination.

First published in 2016 by CalviSu Publishing
ISBN 978-0-9935489-2-5

Website francesfidgetknickers.com

The people I would like to thank:

Well, I can only think of one person, and that is you for buying my book. I'd like to leave it there, but if I did no one would help me with my next story. So here goes. Firstly, my wife for putting up with me … BOY … she's got a heart of gold … and I should say … she is the boss! Then there are my son and daughter, Scott and Nikhaela Wicks. How did I manage to have two such wonderful children? The editing and proofreading were done by Vicki Sennett of Fool-Proofs. She's very good at it – she needs to be with all the spelling mistakes I make! I mustn't forget Dan McCloskey, who, along with my outstanding contributions, managed to dull down my pictures, which I gave him to rework. Just in case you're in any doubt as to how wonderful my drawings are, check out the pictures below.

Neither of these pictures are in the book … but you get the idea of how brilliant my drawings are!

iii

For Su Wicks…

…how lucky I am to have met you.

CHAPTER 1

THE TIGGLE-TROTTER

It was no good.

No matter what they did, Granddad Sprinkle-Tinkle would not come out of his bedroom. He'd stayed in there sulking for the whole week, until Frances Fidget-Knickers' parents had returned from their holiday.

It had been a year since the tricks had been played on him, but the past year had not changed the horrid old man.

Still meaner than a pack of wolves hunting for their prey, Granddad Sprinkle-Tinkle was nastier than ever. Over breakfast, he had taken great joy in dropping Frances and Mary well and truly IN IT!

The stitch-up was big.

They were now in the back garden.

On bended knees, they had been put to work cutting the grass with a pair of scissors each.

Snip, snip, snip, went the scissors. "I don't believe it," began Mary, snipping away with her trimming device. "Every time I stay over, he drops us right in it … and I'm sure he does it just for fun."

Cutting at the lawn, Frances answered, "He knowingly did this, and now my mum and dad have gone out for the day."

The two girls carried on clipping the lawn. Small patches of grass started to look like a very bad haircut. As they worked away, unbeknown to them, something strange was about to happen inside the cottage.

Without a sound, magical and mysterious forces were at play. Time-shifting movements between worlds opened up and tugged at Granddad Sprinkle-Tinkle.

1

From inside the dwelling, came an unexpected outcry. "Get off me!" the wickedest of grandfathers screamed out of the window, as he kept struggling.

Unfortunately for him, the fight went the wrong way, and he was now down to his waist inside a hessian sack – and then he was gone.

Startled, Mary asked, "What was all that about?"

Taking no notice, Frances replied, "Who cares, when he's landed us with this job?"

"Do you think he's okay?" asked Mary, looking over her shoulder at a swinging light shade through the window. "He could have bumped his head!"

"With any luck, maybe some sense went in with it."

The grass-clipping resumed and Mary Midget-Mouth joked, "We're not that lucky. By the way, I like the new kitchen."

The cottage shook. "I DO LOVE A BIT OF OAK AND SOME NICE GRANITE WORKTOPS," said House.

"House, you're such a clever thing," Mary praised.

With another shake, the cottage rattled. "I FEEL A CHANGE IS COMING. I MUST GO."

Mary's eyes roamed around the garden. "You know, if I didn't know House so well, I'd feel a little spooked right now."

A strange sense of something odd was beginning to be felt. A change in the atmosphere, as it became heavy and cold, pushed at their ears.

"I'm getting goose-bumps," Frances shuddered.

Mary pointed at the treetops. "Me too, and don't you think that's a bit strange?" she shivered.

The air was as still as still could be.

There was no wind.

Not even the slightest of breezes.

The trees that surrounded the garden, taller than a three-storey townhouse, began to move.

"That's odd," thought Frances aloud. In an effort to solve the problem, she pondered somewhat. "That is very odd; I wonder what is doing that?"

Unearthly reactions, negative to this world, suddenly took hold. Unfolding before them, a force of immense power hit the trees. Heavy and uncontrolled movements took their branches almost to breaking point as they thrashed about uncontrollably.

Almost at once the branches stopped moving, and out popped Godfrey from beneath the largest oak tree, with a story to tell.

"Good morning Miss Frances and Miss Mary," smiled the rat, dressed in a tracksuit and trainers. "I've just been out for a run." Patting his chest, he puffed, "You know, a bit of keep fit – helps to keep the old ticker going."

It was surprising how Godfrey looked so dashing in anything he wore. Still wearing his monocle and gripping his beautiful cane, he did some star jumps.

Mary asked, "Whatever did you do to the trees?"

Godfrey stopped suddenly. Whiskers twitching, he replaced his monocle before speaking. "It was not me, Miss Mary."

Brisk as you like, the impeccable rat trotted up to the girls, and Frances said, "Very strange – that's never happened before. Without the wind, how do trees move like that?"

His eyepiece positioned correctly, and doing some deep knee bends, Godfrey went up and down with his explanation. "I was out on my early morning run." He stopped just at the top of a knee bend and smiled, "Not in this world, in the magical one. I could not possibly be seen in this world. In this world, rats get killed as vermin."

"I suppose they do," agreed Frances Fidget-Knickers, "and it would look very odd for people to see a rat dressed in sportswear."

"Quite right, Miss Frances," acknowledged the rodent with a nod, as he carried on with his explanation. "There I was, jogging along in the magical world, when who should come along? None other than my dear friend, Mr Tiggle-Trotter."

"Who?" asked the two girls loudly.

Pressing a finger to his lips, the rat stressed, "Now then, not so loud, Miss Frances and Miss Mary. He is behind the trees waiting to come out. Tiggle-Trotters are very shy folk, and we need to go through the proper introductions." Pressing home his meaning, Godfrey insisted, "You will need to be on your best behaviour … and no scaring him away."

4

Frances and Mary stood perfectly still.

"That will do nicely," smiled Godfrey.

Turning round to face the trees, he called out, "It's alright, there's nothing to be afraid of … you can come out now!"

With that, the branches were moved aside as if they were nothing but twigs, and out came the giant.

He was big.

He was bigger than big.

He was the biggest of big you could possibly imagine.

The Tiggle-Trotter towered over the treetops. Up he stood to his full height, leaving the very tops of the branches just under his chin.

Feelings of fear swept over the two girls, for Frances and Mary had never seen such a thing; the Tiggle-Trotter looked like a giant ape.

Thoughts of being squished flatter than a pancake came to mind, as Frances and Mary stayed very still.

"There you are," smiled Godfrey. "That's much better now we can see you."

The giant ape nodded.

Godfrey began with the introductions. With the politest of voices, he started, "Miss Frances and Miss Mary, this is Mr Tiggle-Trotter."

With the lack of acknowledgement from both girls, the giant ape became slightly restless. His manner was beginning to change.

The rodent looked around at them both. "Miss Frances and Miss Mary, you need to nod your heads," he stressed.

So that's what they did.

With a sigh, Godfrey carried on. "Mr Tiggle-Trotter, meet Miss Frances Fidget-Knickers and Miss Mary Midget-Mouth."

The giant ape gave a very meaningful nod of approval and smiled. With the nodding of heads out of the way, he spoke. "I have two letters for you, Miss Frances Fidget-Knickers."

Frances instantly warmed to the giant primate, for he spoke so softly and ever so politely that it made her realise that this huge beast wasn't a wild animal. Intrigued by this, she stood her ground.

A giant hand came down and in it were the two letters. "For Frances Fidget-Knickers, from Judge-Get-It-Wrong. The other is from Mrs Give-Us-A-Giggle."

The letters looked tiny between the fingers of a hand the size of her dad's car.

Mary backed behind her friend, rather worried.

6

Still, Frances did not move, as the enormous arm with the enormous hand at the end of it came towards her.

The enormous arm stopped.

"You can take them," smiled Godfrey, patting the ape's little finger. The little finger was bigger than the rat, as he went on, "It's perfectly safe, and that's why we had the proper introductions." The finger-patting turned to a gentle stroke. "My, it would be a different kettle of fish without them."

The letters appeared to be like small pieces of confetti in the giant's hand, as Mary asked, "What would have happened, then?"

"You would never have got the letters – he would have run away," answered the rodent.

Curiously, Frances took them.

Instantly, one of the envelopes began to wriggle.

It jumped up and unfolded.

Out popped some images.

It was like watching a huge television screen.

One image was that of a bullfrog, and the other a tall insect.

"How cool is that?" gasped Mary, impressed, forgetting her worries about the giant ape. "The bullfrog looks a bit fatter; Judge-Get-It-Wrong has put some weight on, and the solicitor, Mr Never-Won-A-Case, has lost some."

The letter began to speak. "My dear boy, where was I?" said Judge Get-It-Wrong, starting to wave his arm. "Damn! Blast!" croaked the judge, ruffling up all the paperwork as he kept trying to hit a fly. "I'll get you, then that will be the last thing you will be doing." He huffed disapprovingly and insisted, "How dare you come into my chambers without an appointment?"

"Quite right," agreed Mr Never-Won-A-Case.

Splat went the fly.

"Ha-ha, got you!" exclaimed the judge, knocking the fly for six. Admiring his own effort, he stated, "Pretty good batsman in my day, I can tell you!"

"Well done, Your Honour, but we have more urgent matters to attend to," said the solicitor, who suddenly span around to become his alter ego. "Sixes all around and the crowd go wild – three cheers for Judge Get-It-Wrong!" Then, on the tips of his toes, he rotated back the other way and became himself once more, while taking up his seat.

"Too kind, far too kind, my dear chap," smiled Judge Get-It-Wrong, humbly accepting the praise.

"Not at all, Your Honour."

Leaning forwards, the judge declared, "Mr Never-Won-A-Case, you are one of the finest, if not the best, legal minds we have. Give it to me straight."

The solicitor stood up with a spin. Now upright, like a soldier standing to attention, he had turned back into his alter ego. "It's not good news, Your Honour: Snogg-Snifflers all around at twelve, three, six and nine o'clock. We are completely surrounded and outgunned." After the statement, he twisted around and settled into his normal self.

Mishearing Mr Never-Won-A-Case, the judge puffed disapprovingly. "Bog-Lickers – why would anyone want to stick their heads down a toilet?"

"No, Your Honour, I believe it was Snogg-Snifflers," stated the solicitor, correcting the judge.

This time hearing him correctly, Judge Get-It-Wrong cried out, "What? We will have to put a stop to that!" Leaning a little further forwards, and without a clue of what to do, out popped a question. "How do you think we should go about it?" enquired the bullfrog.

"Well, Your Honour, I believe you will need to write three permits."

"As many as that?" puffed the judge, disgruntled by the workload.

"Yes, Your Honour," came the reply.

"That's a lot of paperwork," huffed Judge Get-It-Wrong, rummaging around on his desk. "Why so many?"

"One is for a Miss Frances Fidget-Knickers and one is for a Miss Mary Midget-Mouth."

In a rage, the bullfrog slammed down the fly swatter and left it where it lay. "I remember them – they're criminals!"

"No, Your Honour, they were acquitted," smiled Mr Never-Won-A-Case, reminding the judge.

"So they were," the judge sighed, calming down with a long breath of air. Searching over the desk for the correct documents, he praised the solicitor. "Fine bit of legal work you did there, my boy." Finding the correct papers, he enquired, "What's the other one for?"

Instantly, the reply came back. "Mrs Give-Us-A Giggle," answered the solicitor, admiringly.

"It's an unusual request," said the judge, wanting to know more. "Sending stuff back, are we?"

"Yes, Your Honour," replied the solicitor. "They'll need as much help as they can get when they arrive here."

Judge Get-It-Wrong sniffed. "I'm not having them come back here," he insisted. Picking up the flyswatter and hitting the desk in disgust, he added, "I'm not a babysitter!"

"No, Your Honour, it was merely a figure of speech."

"That's ok, then," huffed the judge, writing out three permits and handing them to the solicitor.

The images of the bullfrog and the tall insect flickered and faded away.

"No reading," yelped Mary happily. "Now that's what you call a letter!"

"I wonder what the other one is about?" asked Frances.

The second letter wiggled and opened in a cloud of smoke. Through the foggy haze, a voice sounded out. "Hello, me dears," it said, as the misty smoke disappeared.

There was no image; only the voice.

Immediately, the two girls chirped in surprise, "Mrs Give-Us-A-Giggle!"

"Sorry you can't see me, I feel a little washed out," explained the voice of the white witch.

"Perhaps she's under the weather?" suggested Frances.

"Can white witches get ill?" Mary asked.

Godfrey quickly insisted, "No time for explaining, let's see what she has to say."

"Me dears," said the invisible Mrs Give-Us-A-Giggle, "I've popped a few things into this wooden box for you. They will come in very useful in times of need. Just tap it and give your instructions and the box will do the rest."

The letter ended in a fizzle, crack and bang of exploding fireworks.

When the smoke had cleared, a wooden box with no lid sat at Frances Fidget-Knickers' feet.

"Let's see what's inside," Mary said eagerly.

Frances picked up the receptacle and gave it a tap.

Nothing happened.

Tipping it upside down, she peered inside the box. "Do you think she's forgotten to pack whatever it was she was sending?"

"Miss Frances," smiled Godfrey, "Mrs Give-Us-A-Giggle said 'in times of need'. At this moment, do you need anything?"

"No."

Mr Tiggle-Trotter spoke. "Hold on to it tightly – both your lives may depend on it, for there are sure to be dangers along the way."

For Mary, there was something remarkably unsettling about the word "dangers". "Hang on a minute, that sounds a little dodgy – we're not coming … are we?" she asked.

In a worried tone, Frances agreed. "Whatever it is, it doesn't sound very good."

Godfrey joined in with a tense look on his face. "Miss Frances and Miss Mary, you can't go against a court order. If you do, Judge Get-It-Wrong will imprison you in Stinkers Prison."

The biggest of apes pinched his nose in front of them. "Once you've paid Stinkers Prison a visit, the stench never leaves you."

"Is that true?" asked Frances.

"Never ever?" gasped Mary.

"That's true, never ever," insisted Godfrey. "Well, what's it to be?"

The two girls had a bit of whispering time. When they had finished, Frances Fidget-Knickers answered, "We're in."

"Splendid," smiled Godfrey. Addressing the huge ape, he said, "Over to you, my dear friend."

The giant primate bent down to just above his waist and began a line of questioning with Frances Fidget-Knickers.

"Have you seen anything strange?"

"Like what?"

"Anything out of the ordinary?"

"Nope."

"Have your parents been acting differently?"

"Not at all."

"What about your grandfather?"

"He's still the rotten old toad he's always been."

Then the next question hit home. "What about any unexpected noises?"

11

"Yes!" spluttered Mary, cutting in. "A few minutes ago there was a lot of banging and crashing inside the cottage."

Two eyes bigger than dustbin lids looked over to the beautiful dwelling. "House, I sense that voodoo has been at work."

With a shake, the dwelling spoke. "IT'S TRUE; THE POSSESSORS OF SOULS HAVE TAKEN HIM. THE SNOGG-SNIFFLERS HAVE GRANDDAD SPRINKLE-TINKLE NOW."

"Oh my, that's very bad news," gasped Godfrey, twitching his whiskers. "Granddad Sprinkle-Tinkle has been … ABDUCTED!"

Starting with a dance, Mary celebrated. "He's out of our lives! No more horrid ways! No more smelly armpits! How can that be bad news? Tell me why, as my hands reach out in joy!"

Uneasily, Mr Tiggle-Trotter answered. "The Snogg-Snifflers are vile creatures. Nasty is what they admire best. Given half a chance, they will destroy my world, and then they will use Granddad Sprinkle-Tinkle to get to this one."

Godfrey flicked through the court papers. "Miss Frances and Miss Mary, it's just as well you agreed to help. I think you should read the permits."

Mary stopped having her joyful moment and studied the documents with her friend. Both permits were the same apart from their names, and they read:

"IN THE PRESENCE OF HIS HONOUR, JUDGE GET-IT-WRONG, YOU ARE DEEMED RESPONSIBLE FOR THE RECAPTURE OF THE WICKEDEST OF GRANDFATHERS, OTHERWISE KNOWN AS GRANDDAD SPRINKLE-TINKLE. FAILURE TO TAKE HIM BACK TO YOUR WORLD WILL BE MET WITH THE PUNISHMENT OF YOU BOTH BEING HUNG, DRAWN AND QUARTERED."

Remembering Miss Know-It-All, her history teacher at school, who had taught the class all about medieval executions, Mary cringed. "Hanging you till you are nearly dead. Laying you out on a table and cutting open your stomach. Pulling out your insides and cutting you into four pieces … that's not my idea of a good time, I can tell you."

Frances shuddered. "I've grown very attached to my body parts," she shivered, checking her arms and legs. "When do we start?"

"It's already begun," replied the giant ape.

A swirling wind sprung up from nowhere. Circular motions lifted them up into a tunnel.

Then they were quickly swept away.

CHAPTER 2

TRAVELLING

Outside of the tornado, the winds hurtled at tremendous speeds. Powered by formidable whirlwinds, it was spinning faster and faster. The phenomenal forces pushed and pulled, twisting the titanic tunnel as it sped along.

At the very centre, inside the enormous magical funnel made from wizardry, everything was still. Apart from white fluffy cushions made from cloudy vapours to sit on, there was just a single door.

A little door.

The door was no taller than Godfrey.

It opened.

And in came the conductor.

Strapped over his shoulders, a cumbersome metal machine lay on the conductor's belly. "Permits please," he asked officially.

Laying on a bed of air, Mr Tiggle-Trotter stretched out. "Nice and relaxing," he yawned. "This is the only way to travel."

Godfrey searched himself and stressed. "Now where did I put them? No, not that pocket."

"No permits," sniffed the conductor, formally, "then you will have to go back."

The shock of the potential punishments made Frances splutter. "If we go back we will be hung, drawn and quartered!"

Fiddling with his machine, the conductor looked a bit puzzled. "Not sure what that means."

Uneasily, Mary told him, "We'll get chopped up into four pieces."

"Sounds nasty – you should go and see a doctor,"
answered the conductor, struggling with the machine.
"Now, do you or do you not have the correct travel
permits?"

"Here they are," beamed Godfrey, handing them over.

The conductor took them, and ran them past his machine.
It bleeped. "Thank you, all seems to be in order.
Refreshments will be along in a minute or two."

He turned and scurried out of the door.

No sooner had the conductor disappeared, than the door opened again. "Cup of tea anyone?" asked a lady pushing a trolley.

Everyone but Godfrey declined the refreshments. "I'd love one – white with no sugar, please," he said, searching for some money.

"Here you go," said the lady. "It's free to first class passengers." With the rattling of the drinks trolley, she trundled back towards the door. "Must get on, lots more people to attend to."

With the door open, it became obvious how powerful the winds were as they blustered past the opening.

The lady and the trolley were sucked out, as the door slammed shut behind her.

"First class," smiled Godfrey. "You are spoiling us!"

The giant ape stretched out to the longest his body would go. Toes pointing at one end, fingertips pointing at the other, he could almost touch both sides of the room. Bouncing gently on the cloudy cushion of air, he yawned. "As I said, it's the only way to travel."

"Mr Tiggle-Trotter," spoke Frances Fidget-Knickers, trying to get his attention. "Please, sir, I have a question to ask you."

He rolled over and the cloud of vapours wrapped around the giant primate's body. "I like 'sir' and I like 'mister'. Most of all, I like 'please' and 'thank you'." His outstretched arms and legs were brought back and he sat up. "Godfrey, you were right. I think I'm going to get on splendidly well with these two."

Godfrey, the smallest person in the room, had the biggest smile, as he said, "Well, well, Miss Frances, you're a master of politeness. Looks like you have made a friend for life, and Tiggle-Trotters live a very long time."

Mary's thoughts came out with ease. "Please, may I ask how old you are?"

The giant ape's voice became softer and his manner warm. Proudly, he announced, "I will be one hundred and fifty-two years old in a couple of months."

"Blimey!" exclaimed Frances.

"One hundred and fifty-two, is that all?" chuckled Mary, finishing off the last three words jokingly.

"I know, another fifty years and I will be fully grown," declared Mr Tiggle-Trotter with pride. "Now, what was your question, Frances?"

"Snogg-Snifflers," she began to ask. "What are they, because I'd like to know what we are up against?"

"Clever, very clever," smiled the giant ape. "Godfrey was right, you are a smart one." Lying back with arms behind his head, the information was given. "Snogg-Snifflers are primitive beasts with humungous appetites. They are very strong. They have poor eyesight, but an acute sense of smell. There is no way of fooling a Snogg-Sniffler's snout."

"Snouts – are they pigs?" Mary blurted out.

Mr Tiggle-Trotter shook his head. "Not really. They look more like an overgrown hog." Stretching out a leg, he described the Snogg-Snifflers in more detail. "Like you and me, they stand on two legs. Unlike you and me, they do not have feet. At the bottom of their legs they have two large toes to bear the weight of the creature. These hoof-like horned toes, and their thick thighs, help to support a stocky body. Relative to their size, they have short legs and arms with stubby hands and fingers."

"They don't sound too nice to me," declared Frances.

"Nor me," insisted Mary.

Godfrey got up and paced up and down, with his monocle held tight in one hand. Every now and then his whiskers would frantically twitch. When he stopped, he said just one word: "Delinquents!" Then he carried on with the foot marching.

"Dumb ones at best," agreed the giant primate, and he carried on with his description. "They have no idea how to speak properly. They are about the height of an average human man. Luckily for men, that is all they have in common, for they are very ugly with large heads."

Godfrey came to a halt with his whiskers twitching like never before. "Let's not be forgetting the powerful jaws that like to crush, grind and gobble us rats down. I would really like to pull out their tusks and show them a thing or two – not that they'd see much with their beady little eyes."

"They have tusks?" asked Frances

Mr Tiggle-Trotter's nostrils flared. Then they relaxed, and he answered, "When they become adults, only the male Snogg-Snifflers' lower canine teeth grow into tusks."

"And the females don't look any better – at best, repulsive with their wiry fur," Godfrey said, sticking his finger down his throat. The rodent gagged. "They're gross."

"I couldn't agree more," laughed the giant ape, "but over time the Snogg-Snifflers have adapted to any terrain, taking advantage of any foraging resources. They have grown strong. There are many. Their success, if you can call it that, comes from being omnivores."

"Omnivores," puzzled Mary. "Whatever does that mean?"

Frances Fidget-Knickers' brain receptors fired away to retrieve the knowledge. "It means that they can eat both plants and animals."

"Correct," smiled Mr Tiggle-Trotter. "I see you have an appetite for learning?"

At those precise words, Mary proudly announced, "Just like the Snogg-Snifflers' appetite for eating, Frances reads a lot of books."

"Well, if that is so, I must show you my collection," smiled the giant ape. "I have a library at home. Would you like to see it?"

Frances gasped in surprise, for she had never met anyone with more books than she had. Finally, she spluttered, "You have your very own library?"

"Yes."

Mary rolled her eyes and sighed. "I thought school was out for the summer holidays!"

Mr Tiggle-Trotter got to his feet. "Life is a journey of learning all in itself, and it looks like we are coming to the end of this one."

The bewitching winds slowed and came to a stop.

Touchdown over and done with safely, all four were now standing in the magical word.

"Not much to see around here," stated Mary Midget-Mouth, viewing the desert. "It's nothing but sand for as far as I can see."

The giant ape pointed into the distance. "You see those mountains that look like little specks on the horizon? That is where we are going."

"My dear friend, that's a very long way," insisted Godfrey, looking over the vast distance. "Would you mind, Mr Tiggle-Trotter, taking one step forwards?"

One foot longer than a double decker bus lifted up and out and onwards. "I'm a bit lost as to what you are doing," commented the giant primate, as the following foot settled down.

Pacing between the giant footprints, the rodent replied, "All will become clear; just give me a few minutes."

Frances and Mary watched him scurrying over the sand until he was beside the furry foot that had stepped forwards – which was quite some distance away. "Miss Frances and Miss Mary, would you mind coming over to me?" he called out. Counting each step until they got to him, the rat muttered, "That will never do."

"Why won't it?" asked Mary.

Worrying about the dilemma in front of them, Godfrey began to explain. "I've taken forty steps, and you have taken twenty, to just one of Mr Tiggle-Trotter's footsteps."

Frances quickly did the maths. "There's no way we can all keep up. We'll fall behind."

The giant ape leant down, holding out the biggest hand Frances and Mary had ever seen. "I can carry you, if that helps?"

Warmly appreciating this gesture of goodwill, Godfrey sighed with relief. "What a good idea! All aboard, Miss Frances and Miss Mary."

Once safely inside the hand, it went up. "We are heading beyond those mountains," said Mr Tiggle-Trotter. "There is a passageway through them. Get some rest – it will be a while before we get there."

Frances Fidget-Knickers relaxed and sighed, with her reluctant rescue in the forefront of her mind. "I wonder where my grandfather could be."

CHAPTER 3

THE KING OF THE SNOGG-SNIFFLERS

The forest was thick with trees. Like a sack of potatoes, the horrid old man had been bagged. A burly Snogg-Sniffler carried him over his shoulder.

"OUCH!" yelped Granddad Sprinkle-Tinkle, as he went bouncing up and down.

"Stop with your complaining," said the muscle-bound brute, slinging the wickedest of grandfathers onto the other side of his body.

"Ouch, me poor old bones," winced Granddad Sprinkle-Tinkle.

The heavy-set beast adjusted himself with a hoisting movement. As the sack came crashing down, he grunted, "I is thinking I is a bit more comfortable now."

"Me poor old stomach!" complained the horrid grandfather as he landed.

It was pitch-black inside the sack, and all the old man could do was listen.

"Can we eats him?" asked a Snogg-Sniffler, eagerly licking his lips.

With a poke, the boar holding the bag of old bones snorted. "I is not feeling much meat on this one. Not even enough for a snack."

"Ouch, that hurts, stop poking me!" moaned Granddad Sprinkle-Tinkle.

Suggestions started to come thick and fast from the hungry pack. "We could always chop him up and use him for stock," said a voice.

"I is knowing a very good recipe for human fleshy bits," said another.

The suggestions carried on.

22

"Keep with the bouncing and bumping, it makes for good tenderising."

"Don't forget to turn him, that way you is getting in all the nooks and crannies."

"How about we is breaking his bones to let the marrow ooze out?"

By this time, Granddad Sprinkle-Tinkle had fainted from the shock of the thought of being eaten.

Up marched an official-looking Snogg-Sniffler. "I is your commander," he stated, raising a stick. "We is under orders of the King." Tapping Granddad Sprinkle-Tinkle's back, he repeated the orders. "This scraggy bag of old bones is not for eating; anyone who is doing so is under pain of death."

Puzzled mumbles started.

"I is not liking pain."

"I does hate it when my knees get grazed."

"I is trembling when nurse Sniffler does put stinging liquid on my cuts."

They all winced.

Then someone said, "What is this death like?"

And someone else answered, "I don't know, I has never tried it."

Some tummy noises were heard and alternative suggestions were voiced for satisfying their hunger.

"What about a nibble as he won't miss his toes?"

"No nibblings."

"What's if we just bites off some fingers then?"

"You is doing no finger-biting, either," huffed the commander. "We is taking this one back all in one piece."

A complaint came forwards from the ranks. "Why is we having to take the long way around?"

Huffing and grunting, the commander said sternly, "You is always with your complaining! I is under orders not to be followed!"

23

The moaning Snogg-Sniffler moaned some more. "I is having aching legs. How much further is we having to walk?"

"Stop with your whinging," huffed and puffed the commander. "We is nearly there – look, see?"

Pushing through the densely packed forest, the area of vegetation opened into a small clearing.

Before the weary group of travellers was a cave.

Into it they marched.

The cavern was vast.

Cylinder-shaped rocks came out of the ground.

Overhead, more cylinder-shaped rocks came down from the ceiling.

The stalagmites and stalactites were large and pointed.

Soon they were entering an enormous underground chamber; in it stood the King's castle, built from stone.

"We is home," sighed the commanding Snogg-Sniffler wearily, as they all disappeared inside the fortified structure.

Granddad Sprinkle-Tinkle was thrown to the ground with a thud.

He didn't move.

"Wake up!" bellowed the large brute who had been carrying him.

Again, he didn't move.

"You is not staying there when you is about to meet the King!" screeched the brutish hog with a kick. "Ups you is waking!"

The old man groaned and woke up, with the deep baritone voice of the King greeting his ears.

"I is having order!" shouted the King, holding onto a lump of meat.

All the unruly beasts stopped with their fighting.

"Apologies, Your Kingship," snivelled a very ugly-looking hog, who had seen far better days. The scars of many battles sliced into his face, he went on, "You is needing some help?"

Their monarch snorted. "I, the King, is having a court crier for speaking, and you is not being him."

The ugly Snogg-Sniffler went down on all fours and grovelled, "Great Sovereign, I is begging your royal forgiveness."

The King sniffed a regal sniff. "You is lucky – lucky I is in good mood. Where is the court officer for making my announcements?"

Silence hushed over the great hall.

All the beastly behaviour stopped as they started to look around at each other. Low sounds of Snogg-Sniffler murmurings whispered out.

"Is you knowing?"

"I is not knowing."

The uneasy shuffling of horned feet, mixed with the muttering sounds of worried Snifflers, kept coming.

"He won'ts like it."

"We is in for the chop."

"I has grown accustomed to my head."

With the loudest of bellows, the king boomed, "Why is I having to wait?" Menacingly, he peered through his tiny little eyes and bellowed out again, "You is not looking hard enough! I is relieving someone of their bonce! A bit of lessening of weight might be making you look harder!"

There were looks of panic, and a horrified silence stilled the air. This terrifying silence was broken by the sound of snoring.

"I has found him!" came a shout from the very far end of the great hall, followed with, "He is sleeping!"

The King stood up and waved the joint of mutton. "Wake sleeping Sniffler up," he commanded.

At once, they did what their king had ordered.

The sleeping Snogg-Sniffler was kicked and punched.

He was then picked up overhead and thrown to the front before the King's feet.

In a sleepy voice, the court crier reported for duty. "I is at your service, Oh Great One," he yawned.

Standing proud and tall, his majesty instructed, "You is speaking after me so all can hear. I is wanting it boom-banging loud."

Up stood the Snogg-Sniffler, not but two steps away. Clearing his throat with a deep, gurgling cough, the phlegm rolled down the back of his mouth. Then he gurgled, "Me talking bits is all lubricated. I is ready, Your Majesty."

Now standing directly in front of his subjects, the King began. "I is thinking."

26

The court crier opened his mouth and out came a booming cry that shook everyone. "Our emperor is having a thinking moment!"

His royal teeth sank down into the joint of mutton. As soon as they did so, meat juice spurted out and dribbled down the King's chin. Savouring the flavour, he declared, "I is still having my think."

Sucking in a huge breath of air, the announcer of words bellowed, "Our kingly one is still having his royal thinking moment!"

His Majesty drew a forearm across his snout and, with a warm and lovely feeling in the pit of his stomach, he stated, "Me thoughts are … yum, yum, better off in me tum."

"Our magnificent one's thoughts are," bellowed the court crier, before filling his lungs and bellowing even louder, "yum, yum, better off in our mighty one's tum-tum!"

There was an almighty stamping of hooves and clapping of hands as all the Snogg-Snifflers celebrated the royal speech.

With the excitement becoming too much, there came rejoicing cheers.

"Our Kingness is right!" yelled a rather skinny Sniffler with half his fur missing.

"He is always right, I is saying!" shouted out a rugged-looking boar.

Overexcitedly, a very fat hog screamed, "We is having the best king ever!"

After which, all the creatures started to bish and bash each other with whatever they could find.

Before his almightiness sat back down, the half-eaten lump of meat was thrown away. Then he stated, "You is bringing Him in now."

CHAPTER 4

DEAL-MAKING

Head to waist covered in a cloth sack, a quivering Granddad Sprinkle-Tinkle was marched in to see the king of the Snogg-Snifflers.

Stumbling to a grinding halt, the old bag of bones shook like a trembling leaf.

"You is taking that off," instructed the King, pointing to a Snogg-Sniffler guarding the trembling wreck. "I is not having talks with a sack of spuds."

Off came the sack, and two squinting eyes looked out. Before him sat the king of the Snogg-Snifflers, in a large, wooden chair carved with the battles of past victories.

"You is Him?" enquired the supremely powerful one.

Shakily, the old man stuttered, "Well, it depends on who you mean by 'Him'?"

The absolute ruler laughed. "You is a cunning one!"

Nervously quivering, Granddad Sprinkle-Tinkle muttered, "I don't know what you mean."

Sniffing the air, the King stated, "You is most definitely Him. My eyes may not be what they used to be, but my smelling is still perfect."

Defeat loomed as the selfish excuse of a grandfather made one last stand. "I could have been standing next to whoever it was you are looking for. Perhaps you are mistaken?"

"Nonsense – you is Granddad Sprinkle-Tinkle," insisted the King, and then he asked, "I am right, you is Him?"

The old man shook in fright so much that his knees knocked together like a pair of Spanish maracas. "I is – I mean, I am Granddad Sprinkle-Tinkle," he stuttered.

28

With a sniff, his mightiness lent forwards and tapped his snout. "I knew it," he grunted.

A desperate yelp came from the frightened old man. "Please don't eat me!"

In amusement, the King licked his fingers and laughed. "Eating you!"

"Please, please, please show mercy," stuttered Granddad Sprinkle-Tinkle. "I don't taste that good."

"Snogg-Snifflers like with the crunching and crushing of bones," chuckled his highness, who had now turned his attention to another joint of meat, "until they are grinded into bite-sizes." Now sniffing, he finished, "Smells good."

Feeling sure he was about to be a meal for the beast in front of him, the wicked old man gasped, "How, why, what have I done to deserve this?"

By now, an enormous joint of mutton had been presented to the King. Holding it in one hand, and supporting it with the other, he ignored the gasping old wreck. "Sprinkle-Tinkle, you is clever!" munched the royal hog.

A cowering Granddad Sprinkle-Tinkle dropped to his knees, praying silently for forgiveness.

Up stood the King, as he went on, "We is needing help and you is giving it."

Now gazing up, with arms out in disbelief, the old man cried, "A life of servitude in handcuffs and shackles – I'm to become a slave!"

Taking one step forwards, with his tongue licking his lips for all to hear, the King spoke some more. "You is full of brains, and I is liking brains."

The worst grandfather ever brought his arms down and held them in prayer. "Only the righteous are made to suffer. You are going to work me to death and then eat me best bits," he squirmed.

"I is not."

"You're not?" gasped Granddad Sprinkle-Tinkle in surprise.

Lip-sucking the bone, his mightiness slurped off the meat and insisted, "No, I is not working you till you is dead, and eating you up. Intelligence you is having? Intelligence we Snogg-Snifflers is lacking. You is full of brainy-knowing facts, is you?"

With the realisation that he was not to be eaten or served as a slave, and after a surprised gape of shock, the horrid old man quickly replied, "I am."

The King smiled.

And with that, Granddad Sprinkle-Tinkle began to lie. "I'm loaded with more brains than I know what to do with; comes from me being sent to the best schools in the land."

By now, the great hall had filled up with around two hundred Snogg-Snifflers, eagerly awaiting their monarch's afternoon speech.

"I is happy to hear you is brainy," smiled the King. "You is having whopping thoughts all the time?"

"ABS-O-STONKING-LUTELY!" Granddad replied confidently. Taking the chance to save his skin, he lied some more. "In me younger days, I invented the pointy things, like a spear, arrow head, dagger, sword and a few other things."

"That's impressive," beamed the King. "Is you inventing the axe?"

"Yes, bit of an off-day, what can I say?" the old man cackled.

The King felt comforted by the old man's lies. "You is shushing up," he said. Now he turned to his court crier and instructed him to come over. "You is repeating after me."

The shouter of words hurriedly put down what he was doing and stood by his monarch.

His mighty one, the ruler of all the Snogg-Snifflers, addressed the crowd. "Did I not be telling you?"

With a grunting intake of air, the court officer bellowed out, "Telling you, the King did!"

Excitedly, the established one held up the joint of meat and declared, "It is Him. We is having voting time now."

Again, the court crier yelled at the top of his voice, "The King says he is Him! You is all making votes for Him joining us!"

At the chance of being in the service of the King, Granddad Sprinkle-Tinkle was caught completely unawares. But no one took any notice of his objections, as two hundred beasts were split down the middle.

The monarch spoke. "We has brute strength but lacking in brains. We is needing someone with ideas."

31

Booming out, the bellower of words repeated, "Strength is being what we is having! But we is having no brainy Snogg-Sniffler! Ideas is what we is needing!"

One hundred Snogg-Snifflers stood either side of the room, drawing in their breaths and snorting it back out through flared nostrils.

"Let the voting begin," instructed the King.

And for the last time, the court crier shouted, "By command of the King, you is all making your votes now!"

As those last words faded, all two hundred beasts began scraping their hooves into the ground. Both sides charged forwards with thunderous, crunching blows as bodies smashed together in the centre of the room.

A voice was heard. "No punching – we is having diplomatic vote."

As pushing and shoving turned to grabbing and gripping, which turned to pushing and pulling until bodies started to tumble to the floor, the King said enthusiastically, "This is being a good vote."

"Is it?" asked Granddad Sprinkle-Tinkle in disbelief.

One brutish beast had another in a headlock so tight that his eyes nearly popped out.

"It looks neck and neck at the moment," the King sniffed, interested.

"Is it?" repeated the astonished old man.

32

The King hushed the grandfather from hell. "I is having no time for chit-chat – we is coming to the best bits."

The voting was intense, with all kinds of political tricks taking place. Slapping of faces and pulling of fur, fingers up noses and eyes being poked. Then there was the twisting of arms and legs, as the battering of Snogg-Snifflers carried on for several more minutes until only one was standing.

"I is liking politics," stated the king of hogs. Focusing on the last remaining Snogg-Sniffler, he asked, "Has you decided?"

"We has!" wobbled the creature.

"What does you be deciding?"

"We is wanting brains. Him is in!"

"Splendid news," beamed their monarch in delight.

A relieved Granddad Sprinkle-Tinkle just sighed.

The King looked at the old bag of bones. "You has been accepted into the Sniffler camp." Beaming with official business, he smiled, "We is making mischievous behaviour together. What is you saying on that?"

Those words were like a birthday come early or a Christmas surprise. Nastily, he smiled, "I like it very much. You can count me in."

Loud cheers filled the air as the Snogg-Snifflers who had been voting got to their feet. And, as Snogg-Snifflers do, they started fighting in celebration.

"Stop with the celebrating!" shouted the King.

The whacking and smacking stopped at once.

His regal finger pointed over the heads of two hundred blood-stained beasts. "Bring in the food," he instructed. "You is all joining me and our new recruit in feasting!"

Granddad Sprinkle-Tinkle looked on as all the Snogg-Snifflers rejoiced with grunting as the banquet began.

As soon as the grub was laid out, there was barging and shunting for the best seats as they sat down.

"I is dog-hungry!" shouted a Sniffler.

"Has they got woofers on the menu?" asked a fat, repulsive beast. "I is liking dog, especially the hind quarters."

"If they has bow-wow," screamed an excited hog, "I will be wolfing down the innards! Liver and kidneys is my favourites!"

A skinny-looking grunter yelled out, "I can't satisfy my hunger. I is munch-gobbling, but it does not be working!"

The munching hog next to him tossed his plate to one side and grunted, "You is calling that scoffing? I is calling it nibbling. Why is you not packing it in, like what I does?"

"I is not jam-packed!" cried the skinny Snogg-Sniffler. "I is thinking I is needing some help!"

With that, two brutish beasts got up and held open the skinny hog's mouth.

"Ram it in!" said one.

"Wedge it down!" said the other.

The skinny hog lay there with his mouth wide open and in went two roast chickens, ten apples, five unpeeled bananas, three dozen boiled eggs and a loaf of bread.

Greedily, he swallowed it all down without chewing. "I is most grateful," he burped.

Realising they were missing out on their feasting time, one of the brutes huffed, "You is scoffing all the grub!"

Returning to their seat, the other porker added, with a disgusting sniff, "We does not be missing out on our grub-munching!"

Then they sat down and gobbled up the goodies on offer.

Engrossed in the eating, a cry echoed out from the King. "Feast on!"

And with that order, it became more extreme. Two hundred Snogg-Snifflers and the King gorged themselves.

In shock, Granddad Sprinkle-Tinkle gazed at them.

Grasping hands grabbed at any morsel. Ravenous appetites devoured everything in sight. With unquenchable thirst, tankards of beer and goblets of wine were guzzled down without coming up for air. If anything was spilled, it was rooted from the floor and licked bare.

There was no resting, when there suddenly came a throat-curdling cry. "You is obstructing my dinner!" snorted a one-eyed swine. "I is famished and you is in my way!"

As if it couldn't get any more out of control, all the Snogg-Snifflers started fighting over the last scraps left on the table.

"I has been thinking," belched the King. "We is always short of food. I has heard of places where there is lots of the stuff. Is you knowing about farms?"

A cunning and wicked smile came over the old man's face. "Farms, you say," he said deviously.

"You is knowing about these places of plenty?"

"Certainly," grinned the cunning old man. "I know all there is to know about farms."

"What is they?"

With a sly look in his eyes, Granddad Sprinkle-Tinkle informed his majesty, "They're places where there is more food than you could possibly imagine. They lie to the west and I know how to get there."

"You is brainier than us all put together, which be hugely agreeable," beamed the King, with a pleased smile. "I does inform you, a few days from now we is ransacking, looting and plundering, pinching and poaching, anything in our reach. We is off to pillage all farms to the low-lands. If you is serving me well, you does never go back to that other world you is coming from."

Granddad Sprinkle-Tinkle's eyes lit up.

"You has received the royal welcome. Is you up for the job?" asked the ruler of the Snogg-Snifflers.

"I'm definitely in," hissed the nasty old man, as the orders were given to make ready for pillaging.

"One more thing," whispered the King. "I is letting you into a secret. Along the way, we is getting fresh meat – we has set a trap for Tiggle-Trotter."

CHAPTER 5

MAKING READY

In the passageway of the mountains, two hundred and fifty-one Snogg-Snifflers were beginning to make their plans for trapping the giant ape.

"I is thinking this is being a good place for ambushing," stated the leading hog.

The second in command hovered close to his leader and they exchanged dark glances. "I is agreeing, we is having steep, jagged rock faces. I is not seeing beasty getting away up there."

Bending down to pick up a large stone, their commander made ready to march on. "I is liking this canyon. We does have boulders and rocks as extra weapons." Now standing, he spoke to all his troops. "This is being the place for our trapping. And no fighting – we is celebrating after Tiggle-Trotter's capture. You is all following me with your quick marching."

Walking on, two hundred and fifty-one eager Snogg-Snifflers picked up the pace.

"I is smart commandant. I has been here before. When I was being here, I is sending commandos up either sides of very narrow bit. Look, see up there – they has big mesh waiting as surprise. We is blocking primate off with net."

An interruption came forwards from the ranks. "Head honcho, why is we sending up our best troops?"

The leading Snogg-Sniffler began his explaining. "I is knowing about Tiggle-Trotters. They is very big with lots of fleshy meats on the bone. When we is ready, commando Snifflers will drop down open-weave material behind him. We does block his escaping way – what does you think?"

A mind-prompting reply came out of the blue. "Why does we not drop netting on the ape?"

Embarrassment fell over the commander. "I is not thinking of that," he snorted with discomfort. Turning the embarrassing moment around, he halted the rank and file. "We is here under orders from our king to stop Tiggle-Trotter."

"That's we is!" insisted the second in command. "I is being there when orders were given by our mighty one."

With a stiff upper lip, the commanding officer grunted, "This here is being our supply post. From here we is supplying Tiggle-Trotter meat to our army."

The lower-ranking officer smiled. "Is orders from our top brass … big cheeses is knowing best."

The commander rubbed his belly. "Big cheeses and top brass, commanding officers and kings, we is all the same when our bellies is empty."

There was restlessness within the troops, as the thought of emptiness in their stomachs took hold.

The shuffling discontent was put to rest by their leader. "You is all here to bash Tiggle-Trotter's brains in. If we is successful, we is having ape for supper tonight. You can have a very quick punch-up, if you like."

Apart from the commander and his junior officer, two hundred and forty-nine Snogg-Snifflers had a very quick fighting moment, and then they made their way to the narrowest part of the passageway.

Pulling the second in command to him, the commander pointed up at an overhang. "You is seeing up there – is good spot for Snogg-Snifflers to be jumping on ape. Where be Pick-It, Roll-It and Flick-It, as I is wanting them up on ledge?"

38

With a cranking of his head, the second in command answered. "They is just over there. They is never getting up on ridge. They is useless at climbing."

"Is we having engineer with us?"

"We is."

The superior officer pushed the inferior hog away. "Then you is getting him to solve problem."

"Yes I is, right away, your leadership," he stuttered, falling back.

"Good," snorted the leader of hogs. "We is not having much time to make ready, so you is making it quick and snappy fast."

The lower-ranked officer began his shouting order. "Engineering Snogg-Sniffler!" There was a slight pause, and then he shouted again. "I is ordering you here at once!"

Up trotted the builder of things. Coming to a stop, he saluted. "I is here at your orders for doing my duty."

With an outstretched arm, the ordering hog grunted. "We is having problems. We is needing to get Pick-It, Roll-It and Flick-It up on ledge."

"You is?" sniffed the maker of things.

"No, you is," corrected the pointing Snogg-Sniffler. "You is right now fixing problems."

Agreeing, the engineer turned. "I is, I is problem-fixing right away."

From then on, the master builder of mechanical things took control, and instructed four Snifflers to help. A hefty and cumbersome boulder was rolled into place. Four struggling beasts put a long, thick plank of wood over the rock. It sat balancing in the middle like a giant seesaw.

The commanding Snogg-Sniffler sniffed, snorted and scratched his head, as the contraption was being built. "I is impressed." Having no idea how the machine worked, he asked the engineer, "What is it?"

Twiddling and fiddling, the engineering porker replied, "I has not finished, I has a bit more to do."

Two more pieces of timber, longer than the first, were laid apart on the ground. At the far end, they were pushed together with a wheel in the middle and fixed in place. At the other end, they were spread apart by wedging a smaller piece of timber between them. Lots of hammering held it in place. Over the banging, the inventor of things could be heard to say, "We is almost done." Another two smaller pieces of timber were attached to the rear and finished off with a long rope running over the wheel. And then it was pulled upright. "I has finished now," he declared proudly.

Scratching his head, the commanding officer pondered over the technical marvel. "How is you working it?"

The master builder of engineering wonders came forth, with his high-tech and scientific explanation. "We is putting Snogg-Sniffler at far end. Then we is trying rope around fattest porker at this end. We is then hoisting fatso up as high as we is pulling, all the way to the top of the wheel. When he does be there, we is letting him go, sending grunting Sniffler up into the sky at the other end."

The technological speak worried the commanding Snogg-Sniffler. "I is thinking with me doubts, will it work?"

"I is not testing," answered the creator of industrial machines. "We is best having our tests first."

Squinting and sniff-searching, the leader of beasts selected a candidate. "You is having lucky day. You is having promotion to chief tester."

Getting onto the machine, the chosen one grunted. "I is most grateful. I is doing my best at being upgraded."

Under the instruction of the engineering officer, a rope was tied to the fattest Sniffler.

At the other end of the machine sat the chief tester.

Fifteen struggling hogs pulled up the fattest of beasts.

40

Once at the top, the instruction was given. "You is letting fatty go now."

Fifteen Snogg-Snifflers did as they were told.

Everyone looked on.

Down came the fattest of porkers. With an almighty thud, he hit the wood. Enormous forces drove down the plank and transferred the energy to the other end. Like a rocket, up went the tester.

"This here testing is a piece of cake," he smiled, flying through the air. "Make it a whole one while I is up here!"

Inspecting the airborne hog with great interest, the engineering officer mumbled, "I is liking the look of testing." With a sudden change of his mind, he muttered, "Maybe I does not."

"Splat" went the tester, just missing the ledge as he came crashing to the ground. "I is changing my thoughts about being guinea pig," he winced. Picking himself up and dusting himself down, he staggered back to the contraption. "I is not liking promotion," he moaned, seating himself for a second go.

Adjustments were made. Improvements with movements took place. Final checks were taken by the prime mover, and then all was ready.

For the second time, the fattest Snogg-Sniffler was pulled up, and for the second time the order was given, sending the chief tester flying like a superhero through the sky. "I is expecting more payments than fatso down there," he sniffed. With a grunt, he landed safely.

The second test was a complete success.

It was a proud moment for the engineering hog, who was shunted aside by the commander. "Chief tester!" he shouted. "You does come back down now!"

Sure enough, the chief tester jumped off the ledge.

He hit the ground with a thump.

He got up.

He complained.

But no one listened.

One by one, Pick-It, Roll-It and Flick-It were tossed into the air and landed safely on the rocky shelf.

"You is having your orders!" shouted the commander.

"We is!" came the shouted reply. "We is jumping on Tiggle-Trotter and smashing him on the head!"

Their leader shouted back. "Those is the correct orders! You is making no noises now! You is our surprise!" He turned to his troops. "We is all hiding now, and you is all shushing like sneaky alligators!"

The contraption was taken to bits and hidden from sight.

All of them hid and waited.

"We is downwind," whispered the second in command, "and Tiggle-Trotter is not smelling us. We is in perfect place for ambushing."

"Yes, we is," hushed his superior officer. "Now we does be waiting."

Up on the ledge, things were getting very boring. The boredom was broken by a bit of finger-wiggling.

"I is getting one," said Pick-It, wriggling out an enormous bogey. "Look, see – I has a whopper."

43

"Give it here," said Roll-It, snatching the lump of snot. "I is giving it a good rolling." The large lump of green slime was rolled between the palms of his hands. "I has finished," he proudly declared, handing it over to Flick-It.

"Impressive – it be a massive one," exclaimed his brother, admiring the snot ball in his fingers. Looking down, he spotted his target. "I is not liking engineering Sniffler with his snooty ways," he commented, and fired the bogey ball down at him.

Speeding through the air, it hit home.

"Ouch!" cried the maker of things. Looking up, he shouted, "When you is coming down, I is having punch ups with you!"

Pick-It, Roll-It and Flick-It ignored his complaining, as their ears pricked up. Hearing something in the distance, they started to sniff. "Shush – Tiggle-Trotter does be coming," they all hushed.

Immediately, there was silence.

As the giant ape came into view, not a single unwanted sound could be heard.

The trap was set.

CHAPTER 6

A SNOGG-SNIFFLER AMBUSH

"We are making good time," said Godfrey, smiling at his pocket watch. "Just over three hours to get here." Studying the natural mass projecting upwards, he gasped, "Oh my, how are we going to get through?"

The mountain face was too steep and too high for even Mr Tiggle-Trotter to climb. Considerable earth-shifting moments in the past had pushed the mountain up above the clouds.

"Over there," answered the giant ape, indicating a gap in the rocks. "That is our way through."

As they went in, even the giant primate looked small. "Talk about high," whistled Mary Midget-Mouth. "There's snow up there."

Mr Tiggle-Trotter began a conversation with Frances Fidget-Knickers; Mary was about to undergo a very detailed learning experience.

"Mountains are important to life," explained the giant primate, "because most rivers begin in mountains."

"That's right, they do," said Frances, inspecting the rock formations. "When two continents collide, complex folds are driven up, creating huge boundaries."

"That's correct," acknowledged the great ape. "Do you know about igneous rocks?"

In an instant, Frances replied, "They're formed from lava or magma, cooling and solidifying."

"What about sedimentary rocks?" asked Mr Tiggle-Trotter.

Instantly a reply came again from Frances. "They are formed when loose sediments on the surface become compressed and bond together. I think these mountains might have once been at the bottom of a sea, many millions of years ago."

Nodding in agreement, Mr Tiggle-Trotter asked, "How about metamorphic rock?"

Effortlessly, Frances Fidget-Knickers answered. "Metamorphic rocks – well, they are rocks whose composition has changed through heat. The chemical processes and pressure mean you can find slate, marble and sometimes even granite."

"She's right," smiled Godfrey, ever so proudly. "Excellent memory, and always studying – that's our Miss Frances for you."

Mary Midget-Mouth sighed. "I don't know how she does it. When I took my geography exam at school, I got a letter sent home from Mr Walk-About. He only went and said my paper was ungradable, the worst he had ever seen." Mary sighed some more and then stressed, "I don't get it – I really tried my hardest and I even studied for it!"

Before they knew it, a crashing sound behind them suddenly echoed out.

The great net had been dropped by the commando Snogg-Snifflers.

There was no way back.

The trap had been sprung.

Behind them, Pick-It, Roll-It and Flick-It stood ready to pounce.

Two hundred and forty-eight Snogg-Snifflers came charging out of their hiding places.

"We has ambushed you!" laughed the commanding porker, looking very pleased with himself.

"HOLY COW!" cried the giant primate, in complete surprise.

"I is not caring if you is being scared!" laughed the commander some more. "I is still eating you all the same!"

From the giant hand of the great ape, Frances, Mary and Godfrey peered over the huge fingertips.

"Tiggle-Trotter!" shouted the commanding Snogg-Sniffler. "We is having you for dinner!" Now noticing the three faces peering down at him, he smiled, "I is seeing you has brought some starters!"

Frances gulped and asked, worried, "Does he mean us?"

There was no time to answer, as Pick-It, Roll-It and Flick-It jumped onto the giant ape's back. With a jolt of surprise, he cried out, "What's happening?"

The three brothers started to climb. "There, there, beasty," soothed Pick-It. "We is climbing to your bonce."

"Calmly does it," sniggered Roll-It. "When we is up there, we is giving you a nice present."

"Steady does it, you freaky giant," chuckled Flick-It. "We is then smashing your head in."

Awkwardly, the giant ape tried to wriggle them free from his body. It was hopeless as the brothers three held on, sensing their victory was near.

Smacking his lips, Pick-It said, "When we is cooking tonight, I is having arm stew and dumplings."

Dribbling with the thought, Roll-It added, "With lots of vegetables."

Drooling with the idea, Flick-It made yummy mouth-watering sounds. "I does like garlic."

The giant ape looked down into his hand, as big as a king-sized bed.

Godfrey noticed it first. "Miss Frances, the box!"

It shook very violently in her hand and then it whizzed around on her palm; at the same time, her voice shuddered out, "I'm not making it happen!"

It slowed.

It stopped.

It now sat perfectly still.

Mary's eyes gazed on as a tiny ant crawled onto the rim, with what looked like an extremely small helmet on its head. It sat down. "Is that it?" she asked, unimpressed.

A note popped out of the box and into Frances Fidget-Knickers' hand.

It spoke. "Hello, me dears," said the voice of Mrs Give-Us-A-Giggle. "Don't forget to give clear instructions."

Without thinking, the rodent rocked back onto the heels of his feet. Correcting his posture, he leant forwards and said, "How very thoughtful. Perhaps you should give it a try, Miss Frances."

Uninspired by the single solitary insect, Mary gave her opinion. "What is one ant going to do against all those beasts down there?"

"Let's find out," Frances answered, giving full and clear instructions while pointing to the enemy. "If you wouldn't mind, could you please attack those nasty Snogg-Snifflers, including the ones on Mr Tiggle-Trotter's back?"

The ant stood up and gave its commands to the box in an insect language no one understood.

At first, the box shook ever so gently, while Godfrey suggested, "I think you should put it down, Miss Frances."

Now sitting on the palm of the giant ape's hand, it rattled with deep-down noises of movement.

"Miss Frances and Miss Mary, I'm not sure what is going to happen, so I think we should all stand back," insisted the rodent, tugging at their clothes.

Just as he said those words, a colossal amount of insects came charging out of the box. They quickly caught up with the leading ant and ran up and over the shoulder of the giant primate and into battle.

"Bless my soul," gasped Godfrey. "They're army ants!"

The line of insects never broke, resembling swarms of unstoppable locusts. There were so many that it was impossible to know their true number.

Pick-It, Roll-It and Flick-It got the shock of their lives, with the biting sensations as the ants swarmed over them.

"OUCH! AHHHH! OUCH!" they cried out in pain.

"We is under attack!" shouted the commanding Snogg-Sniffler as Pick-It, Roll-It and Flick-It were sent crashing to the ground. "Squish them under foot, I is ordering you!"

Ten porkers went to the aid of their comrades as the commandos jumped in. They jumped up and down and smashed their fists into the bodies of Pick-It, Roll-It and Flick-It.

The ants were being killed off in unimaginable numbers.

Up on the hand of the giant ape, the box shook, and more ants came rushing out to replace their fallen heroes.

"We is having trouble keeping up with the squishing!" yelled out one of the Snogg-Snifflers, desperately jumping up and down.

At first, another ten roaring boars rushed in to do battle.

It was not enough.

Twenty more raging hogs piled in to do war with their enemy.

Still it was not enough.

The commanding Snogg-Sniffler spotted this and roared, "I is having my thinking – I does send in all of my troops!" Furiously, the leader tugged at the second in command. "I is staying here; I does inspect you is all bashing properly! You is getting on with it now!"

49

"Attack!" boomed the second in command.

With the troops committed to action, they all charged forwards.

Frances, Mary and Godfrey watched the box shake again. Tens of thousands of ants came racing out, inconceivable waves of insects washing over their victims. With bites more painful than picking a splinter out of your finger, they kept on nipping.

The excruciating cries of suffering Snogg-Snifflers trying to do battle with their enemy filled the air. "I is bitten more than I is knowing how to be counting!" screamed an uneducated baconer.

"You is dimwit!" yelped another warty hog, frantically brushing at his fur. "You has not learned how to count!"

"Thicko!" winced another hoggish brute, scratching at his body. "You is runt of the litter, and you is having no schooling!"

All around Mr Tiggle-Trotter's feet, frantic cries and yelps for help sounded out. The Snogg-Snifflers by now were completely covered from head to toe in black army ants, which were very happily biting away at the hogs' bodies.

Up on the giant ape's hand, the box stopped shaking. The last stragglers scuttled up the arm as thick as a tree trunk, then disappeared over the shoulder as wide as a house. Quickly, they joined their comrades.

When the ants were all together, a final wave of pincher-sinking bites took over, and then they suddenly vanished.

Battle-weary Snogg-Snifflers staggered to their feet.

But the worst was yet to come.

As soon as they got themselves upright, they began to lose colour. An uncontrolled churning deep down in the pit of their guts started to happen. Compulsive stomach-wrenching movements took over.

Then all of a sudden, out came the sea of vomit.
They puked to the left.
They puked to the right.
Spewing in every direction, the stomach acid kept gushing out.

The beasts could not speak, for every time they opened their mouths, out came the liquid full of lumps. From the strain of the violent tummy movements, they began to fall over and into the pool of sick. Now on the ground, they chucked up and sprayed fountains of puke all over each other.

"Oh my word, that's nasty!" exclaimed Godfrey, looking down at the defeated Snifflers. "I do believe those ants were using germ warfare."

Seizing his chance to escape, Mr Tiggle-Trotter knelt down. "Get ready and brace yourselves!" he said.

"Miss Frances and Miss Mary, I think we should do as we are told."

"Do you think he's going to make a run for it?" asked Frances.

"Get set," said the giant ape, moving up into a take-off position.

Bracing herself, Mary answered, "Looks like it."

"Go!" shouted Mr Tiggle-Trotter, racing off, his giant leg muscles pushing him free.

Frances, Mary and Godfrey were thrown back with tremendous force.

Upright within seconds, the giant primate picked up speed.

All they heard in the distance was the faint cries of the commanding Snogg-Sniffler. "I is having empty belly! We is all starving tonight!"

They all tried to look over the fingers of the giant hand they were in. The wind cut into their eyes, making them water, so they all sat down with their backs against fingers as thick as telephone poles.

As if on a train journey, they looked out of where the windows would have been. The blur of images were starting to run into one line of colour. With a sudden pulse of energy, they reached full speed and the line of colour turned into an unrecognisable streak.

It was remarkable how comfortable the travelling was as they hurtled along. Only occasionally there would be the slightest of bumps. Every time the slightest of bumps happened, Mr Tiggle-Trotter would apologise for the inconvenience.

Slowly, everything changed from sand to green. Suddenly, the giant ape slowed to half throttle as he gently put the brakes on. With this change in speed, it was impossible to know how far they had travelled.

Then they stopped.

"We are here," he said, catching his breath.

But exactly where was here? thought Frances Fidget-Knickers.

CHAPTER 7

HOME

A shadowy light oozed over the area, with a smell of dampness greeting everybody's senses. The primeval forest was vast, with the undergrowth tangled throughout the ancient woodland. A scattering of fallen leaves hid the dirt, and timbers lay rotting with fungi growing over them.

"Where are we?" asked Frances Fidget-Knickers.

"Home," smiled Mr Tiggle-Trotter happily.

"What a jolly nice place it is," mused Godfrey with a thoughtful look.

Mary searched the forest, staring. "It doesn't look like much of a home to me – where's your house?"

The giant ape tipped his head back. "Up there," he said, tapping a tree trunk.

Gigantic, humongous and immeasurable could not describe the sheer size of the tree. The trunk stretched up, disappearing out of sight and hiding its branches above the visible mass of condensed water vapour floating high above them.

Mr Tiggle-Trotter raised his hand. "It will be easier if you all sit on my shoulders."

"Ha ha!" cried Godfrey. "Miss Frances and Miss Mary, this will be interesting!"

They climbed off the huge hand. "You will need to hold on tight to my fur."

And that's exactly what they did.

The giant primate took hold of the incredibly thick stem. It was clear to see why his feet and hands were so big. The oversized limbs clung to the tree and the giant ape started to climb. "It might get a bit bumpy," he breathed, beginning their ascent.

Now the two extremely long arms and legs began working with ease. Gripping and releasing in a controlled manner, he effortlessly approached the clouds. With powerful movements, the giant primate climbed through them, and then surged through the misty vapours on the other side.

Frances and Mary wiped their eyes, to take away the droplets of water left on them as they passed through the moisture. As the jungle was left behind under an ocean of mist, they saw branches spreading out over the whiteness of the clouds.

Godfrey shook himself dry.

A mass of folding growth with grass and moss covered the whiteness, making a floor. Overhead, a lemon sun rippled with warmth.

"Home at last – this is my humble abode," Mr Tiggle-Trotter beamed.

It was the biggest home Frances and Mary had ever seen. In front of them stood a wooden palace so large that you could not see where it ended. It was simply colossal, with shrubs, hedges and brambles growing around the bottom of the structure. Thick creepers and vines crept over the wooden dwelling. In some places, the undergrowth was so dense the timbers were lost from sight.

"I see you have finished the extension," smiled Godfrey, admiring the work.

"That I have."

"The bathroom, wasn't it?"

"Yes, it's beautiful – and we do need to clean ourselves up before dinner," replied the giant ape.

Godfrey gave a little sigh of discontent. "If only it was that easy to clean up Granddad Sprinkle-Tinkle's act."

The giant ape jumped over what appeared to be a garden wall half his own height. When he landed, he agreed, "We would need more than soap and water to do that."

Frances, with an awkward look of shame, admitted, "I know my horrid grandfather is a wicked old man …"

Mary joined in with a bit of memory-jogging. "It's not your fault, Frances," she stressed, reminding her friend of the rest of the information. "He did all those nasty things before you were even born." With a squeeze of friendship, Mary reassured her best mate. "And all the evidence has been written down and kept for people to read."

Walking up to a huge door and pushing it open, Mr Tiggle-Trotter asked Godfrey, "How much do they know about Stinky-Tinkle?"

"He who never washes," sniffed the rat. "Only a small fraction of the truth, I'm afraid."

"That's not going to make for pleasant reading," acknowledged the giant primate, entering a maze of passageways.

The main artery to the house took on a life all of its own. It was more like a tropical paradise, with noises of insects and birds busying away their day. Scurrying sounds of rodents busying themselves, working with gnawing teeth, could be heard.

The air had a lovely sweet aroma and Godfrey hung his head in shame. "I've wanted to tell, Miss Frances, but if I break my agreement I will be sent to …"

"You mean there are more crimes he's committed?" asked Frances Fidget-Knickers, annoyed.

With a cringe, the rodent answered, "Absolutely, Miss Frances – and, as Mr Tiggle-Trotter said, it doesn't make for good reading."

"I wonder what they are?" asked Mary, interested.

The great ape sighed. "It's a terrible burden for a rat such as you to carry those secrets around."

"What secrets?" asked Frances.

Opening a door, the route of the conversation was changed. "We can talk more when we have eaten," insisted Mr Tiggle-Trotter. "My bathroom – shall we get ready for dinner?"

"My word!" exclaimed Godfrey, with a tone of genuine admiration. "What a splendid job!"

The bathroom was like no other. It was the height of extravagance. The size of it was simply unbelievable.

"Crikey," gasped Mary, "it's bigger than the swimming pool I take lessons in!"

A sunken bath filled with water, two times bigger than a fifty-metre swimming pool, sat in the middle of the room. To the left sat a smaller bath no longer than the giant ape's feet. Nesting around it were strange-looking birds no bigger than a goose.

"Excuse me, Mr Tiggle-Trotter," said Frances, watching the odd-looking birds. "What are they?"

The giant ape put all three of them down and dived into the enormous bath. When his head popped back up, he answered Frances Fidget-Knickers' question. "Poop-Em-Squiggers."

Mary approached the odd-shaped creatures.

Some of them were green, some of them were orange and some of them were red, but all of them had immaculately kept plumages.

Godfrey unzipped his tracksuit jacket. "Miss Mary, meet the traffic light birds – they're very friendly."

All of the Poop-Em-Squiggers had webbed feet. At the end of their feet were small claws. They had a u-shaped body, with what appeared to be a head at either end.

The clipping sound of claws on tiles was heard as a couple of Poop-Em-Squiggers made their way towards Mary.

She held out her hand. "Hello there, do you want a bit of fussing?"

Instantly, the giant primate roared with laughter. "You're talking to the wrong end!"

"Is she?" asked Frances Fidget-Knickers, her very kind mind wanting to learn more. "Can you tell us about them?"

Again, Mr Tiggle-Trotter laughed. "Poop-Em-Squiggers walk backwards. All you will be getting from that end is a nasty mess, and a smelly one at that."

Mary's cheeks flushed brightly as she defended her mistake. "How was I supposed to know?"

Frances, in learning mode, asked more. "Why do they walk like that? I mean, backwards?"

Still chuckling, the great ape answered. "It helps them with finding food." Then he dived out of the water and back in like a dolphin speeding through the sea. He came to a rest just before Frances. "Such an inquisitive mind – asking questions is a sign of intelligence."

So Frances asked another one. "How can that be if the birds are walking away from their food?"

Mr Tiggle-Trotter settled himself and explained. "They scrape away at the dirt while walking backwards to expose insects and small worms. As they do so, they peck at them and guzzle down their findings."

Mary, too, had some questions, which came blurting out. "Why two heads? Why are their feathers that colour? It's a dead giveaway!"

"Miss Mary," smiled Godfrey, "they're very good questions."

The giant ape agreed and revealed his knowledge a little more. "Their way of walking backwards is a defensive ploy, making them appear to be watching out for danger at all times. If that does not work, then the brightly coloured plumage tells predators that they are poisonous to eat."

"That's quite frightening," said Mary. "Some of the things I like to eat have lovely bright colours."

"As long as it's not amphibian," said the great ape, going into more detail. "In your world, there are certain frogs in Central and South America that are brightly coloured. This is a warning sign to other creatures that they are toxic with deadly poisons, and not very good to feed on. It's nature's way of saying 'we are off the menu unless you want to croak it'."

Mary panicked, as a Poop-Em-Squigger nestled into her hand. "Will I die?" she screamed.

"Only if you decide to eat it, Miss Mary," smiled Godfrey, reassuringly.

"That you would," warned Mr Tiggle-Trotter. "It's a slow and extremely painful death. But enough of that. Shall we get cleaned up and ready for dinner?"

There was no stopping Godfrey, as he was down to his underwear in ten seconds flat. With a small splash, he popped back up with his head just above the water line. "Come on in – the bathwater is lovely and warm."

In a flash, both girls did the same and followed after the rodent, as the giant ape turned a switch. "I fancy the bubble maker," he said.

An instant sound of motorised movements rumbled out.

The water started to gurgle, and with it a soapy clear liquid of moving emptiness swallowed Godfrey. He was now inside a huge bubble, and he cried out in delight. "This is how bathing should be!"

Frances floated next to Mary. She was quickly taken by one of the soap suds. Now inside the soapy envelope, Frances rose up to meet Godfrey. "This is amazing!" she gasped.

Mary managed to escape a moving mound of bubbling liquid, only to be caught from beneath by a bubble. "I'm not sure about this," she quivered.

Before long, all three were together, gently bopping up and down inside their clear liquid balls.

Godfrey started to run. "It's the only way to move it," he gasped.

Both girls copied him.

Like bumper cars at a fairground, they crashed into each other. On impact, the inflated film of soapiness would burst, sending them all falling back into the bath, only to be picked up by another soapy ball of bubbling liquid.

"Wowee!" shouted Frances-Fidget-Knickers. "This is the best bath I've ever had!"

Normally for Mary, baths were not an enjoyable experience. This had now changed, as she cried out in joy, "What a way to get clean!" Tumbling head over heels, she added, "My mum and dad would think I'd gone quite mad if I kept asking to have a bath like this!"

The instinctive playfulness inside Mr Tiggle-Trotter started to shine through. He swirled his arms around and those very big fingers swished through the water, making even more bubbles.

By now, the bath water was completely covered in a film of soap suds.

Every now and then, pockets of soapy liquid would float up and get squished in the palm of the giant ape's hands. Excitedly, he would blow Frances into Mary, and Mary into Godfrey. Then he would prick the bubble they were in with his finger. "Pop!" it would go, and down they went onto a springy mattress of liquid sponginess, only to be sent up again inside another thin sphere of liquid.

Over and over again this happened.

It got quite mad with excitement at times.

But no one complained, as they were having far too much fun.

The Poop-Em-Squiggers flew up and joined in with the popping of soapy water. Swooping in and out of the foam, they darted up to burst the transparent coverings. Like a rocket exploding, the spraying foam spread out its display, and the Poop-Em-Squiggers would squawk with joy.

The time just seemed to fly by, but unfortunately Mr Tiggle-Trotter's stomach had other ideas. "We need to get out now," he said, patting his middle.

Godfrey sighed. "It seems such a shame to stop while we are having so much fun – just a few more minutes, please?" he pleaded.

"Dinner time," winked the giant ape, "and it's salad."

"Salad, you say," smiled Godfrey. Then he started to run. He ran as fast as his legs would go. Just as he reached full speed, he jumped up and through the bubble. With a splash, he quickly got out of the bath and said, "Why didn't you say? I suppose all good things must come to an end, only for another one to start."

With a tremendous burst of energy, the bubbles were popped for the last time and down the two girls fell. "We're giving this up for a bowl of salad?" muttered Mary, bobbing around in the water.

"Where do you think he keeps the towels?" asked Frances, swimming to the side of the bath.

As they both got out, Mary answered, "I have no idea."

"Miss Frances and Miss Mary, Mr Tiggle-Trotter and I don't use towels," spluttered Godfrey, shaking himself dry. "It's quite easy – why don't you both give it a try?"

Frances Fidget-Knickers and Mary Midget-Mouth shook themselves every which way they could.

It didn't work.

Still soaking wet, they looked like drenched rats.

"Humans," sniffed the giant ape. "They're not very good at drying themselves. Let me show you how it's done." Gyrating his massive frame, droplets of water bigger than water melons shot out in every direction. The shaking went on for around fifteen seconds, until he finally stopped. "There, give it another go," he said, inspecting himself.

Wriggling and wiggling, the girls' attempts failed miserably.

Godfrey stated the obvious. "Mr Tiggle-Trotter, they're still wet."

Standing in a puddle, Frances suggested, "We really could do with some towels!"

There was a look of bewilderment on the giant ape's face. "What are towels?"

"They look like small blankets," said Mary, with soap suds around her feet.

"Whatever is a blanket?" asked Mr Tiggle-Trotter, somewhat puzzled.

"Never mind," said Godfrey, addressing the giant ape. "Did you have the deluxe feature put in?"

"I did – the Poop-Em-Squiggers enjoy it enormously."

"Why don't we use that?"

"We could give it a try."

The two girls were pushed inside a large room with four padded walls. Even the floor and ceiling were cushioned for protection. Then a whooshing sound began and small jets of air pushed out from all sides. Waves of refreshing warm air almost lifted the girls up.

With her checks flapping in the wind, Frances cried, "This is fantastic!"

Mary, trying to brush her hair out from her eyes, yelled excitedly, "It's brilliant – just like an enormous hairdryer!"

The warm air rushed out with ever increasing speed and the force lifted them up.

"It feels nice and cosy," smiled Frances warmly, twisting around and around. "This is better than any towel I have ever used."

With her gymnastic feat of rolling over, Mary did some somersaults. "I wish it was this easy at my gym class."

Frances tucked in her knees and did a forwards roll. She went up into a handstand and said enthusiastically, "Got to make sure all of me gets dry!"

Turning cartwheels, Mary rolled with ease. "If only my gym teacher Mr Flip-It could see me now."

The sound of the air kept on going, with Frances performing more acrobatic stunts. "You'd be top of the class, that's for sure."

Rolling over and over, Mary said gamely, "If I had something like this at home, I don't think you would get me out of here."

All of a sudden, Godfrey opened the door and the sound of the air slowed. "Hurry up and get dressed, Miss Frances and Miss Mary. It's time for dinner now."

CHAPTER 8

A STRANGE SALAD

Dressed and ready, all four were now in the dining room. Given that it was a room for giants, there were no chairs small enough for Frances, Mary and Godfrey to sit on.

"We seem to have a problem," muttered the giant from his seat, while looking down at them standing on the table top in front of him. With a flash of inspiration, he pushed the chair back and declared, "I know – I have some paper somewhere." Rushing to the shelves, he mumbled, "That's too small, they're too thick." In and out his hands searched. Back and forth went his arms. Flicking and weaving went his fingers as he stressed, "No, not in there … where did I put it?" Suddenly, his voice changed with relief. "Found you."

Sitting back down, he began to fold the paper in a most practical way. Exquisitely made chairs from the art of paper folding were placed around a beautifully hand-crafted table. "Here you are – you can sit on these."

Frances tested the chair.

It was very strong and it was very comfortable. "That's clever of you," she chirped approvingly.

"How did you do that?" asked Mary, sitting on her seat.

"Origami," smiled Godfrey. "Mr Tiggle-Trotter has been studying the Japanese art of paper folding for years."

The giant ape put to one side the stack of leftover paper. Bringing his attention back to them, his voice zinged with great interest. "Not just the art, but the history as well – 'origami' is made up of two smaller words."

Frances Fidget-Knickers raced out the meaning. "Ori means to fold and kami means paper. I read it somewhere, but that's all I know."

64

"Then let me go into the history of it all," beamed the giant ape. "In your world, at the beginning of the seventh century, it is believed that paper-making was introduced to Japan from elsewhere in the Asian continent."

"Really?" responded Frances, her keen mind taking in the information. "That's very interesting; please go on."

"Washi, a thin durable paper, was developed by the Japanese people. At first it was mainly used for Buddhist religious writing and official record keeping. Over time, washi was used to wrap offerings to gods in Shinto religious rituals ..." He stopped, a finger tapping at his temple. Remembering the information, he carried on. "During the Muromachi period, I think between 1380 and 1573, the Ogasawara and Isa families established the requirements of social behaviour. Formal folded ornaments became a requirement for paper wrapping. The tradition is still very much alive to this day."

"Well, you're very good at it," smiled Frances, "and these chairs are made beautifully."

Mary had no real interest in the art of paper folding, and she asked, "What's for dinner? I'd really love a bacon sandwich!"

Mr Tiggle-Trotter gasped.

Godfrey nearly fell out of his chair.

Frances and Mary looked on in surprise.

"There's no meat!" gulped the giant ape, with a hand over his heart. "I'm not murdering animals – I'm an honest and honourable Tiggle-Trotter. I try my hardest never to hurt a living thing. In that way, I believe I am on the path to enlightenment."

"You're a Buddhist?" asked Frances.

"No," replied the giant primate, "I'm a vegetarian."

Mary screwed her face up in a puzzled stare, and asked, "A what-a-tarian?"

65

"Miss Mary, Mr Tiggle-Trotter only eats vegetables and fruit, with some nuts mixed in for good measure."

Frances looked at Mary and mouthed silently, "Meat is definitely off the menu."

"What, no bacon?" cried Mary, somewhat appalled.

"No!" snapped Mr Tiggle-Trotter, abruptly.

This was the first time they had sensed a change in the giant ape's manner, as he got up to leave.

Godfrey whispered very quickly and very quietly, "Now then, Miss Frances and Miss Mary, I'm sure you will like something on offer."

Frances leant into Mary, as the giant ape left the room, and whispered, "I don't think it would be wise to upset him."

Mary returned her whispering. "I'll pretend that I like everything he gives us."

"Good for you," whispered her friend. "That should calm him down."

Totally consumed in their private conversation, the two girls were interrupted by Godfrey saying, "I do apologise, Mr Tiggle-Trotter – they're not used to the way of this world, or the many splendid things it has to offer."

Now mentally back in the room, Frances and Mary stared at the giant primate.

In forgiveness, he nodded and smiled at the two girls.

Now standing before them, holding a knife that made his hand look small, he said, "I will chop up some vegetables and fruit, and make them into smaller pieces for you all to eat."

Godfrey cleared his throat with a short cough. "Please, could you crush some nuts while you're at it?"

The knife flashed before their eyes, so fast that it became a blur. "Will do – any particular ones?"

Godfrey answered, his eyes flickering brightly, "My favourites are the fizzy ones, and I'm very partial to the chocolate whizzers."

"I've never heard of them before," said Frances, without really asking a question.

Mary leant over to Frances and spoke softly. "If you haven't, and you come from this world, then I definitely haven't."

Three paper plates were placed on the table top, filled with all sorts of vegetables and fruit. A sprinkling of crushed nuts sat over them like a snow-covered mountain top. "Dig in," smiled Mr Tiggle-Trotter.

Mary looked unimpressed.

Frances accepted hers with enthusiasm. "Thank you very much. Do you have any knives and forks?"

The giant ape's memory flashed back to a time with distant relatives who had long been dead. "My great grandfather and my own father would talk of things, strange things they had seen in your world. On one occasion my father told me a story from when he was no more than ten years old. At that age, we Tiggle-Trotters are only one and a half times taller than a fully grown human man." He looked at them all with eyes lost in the memory, and spoke fondly at the thought. "Being young and inquisitive, he was wandering the Pacific Northwest region of North America, when he spotted some humans for the very first time in his life. He told me they were sitting around a camp fire and using a funny-looking thing – they prodded at their food and up would come a piece sticking on the end of it."

"That's a fork," said Mary.

"Is it now … and the scooping thing they slurp with?" he asked.

"That sounds like my mother with a spoon," frowned Frances disapprovingly.

With the giant ape's pleasant memories swashing around inside his head, he unfolded the story a little more. "Having no knowledge of humans, he just walked up and took one of those slicing what-you-may-call-its, and carried on walking through the beautiful forest. But these humans took fright and chased him away."

"That's humans for you," insisted Godfrey. "All they ever want to do is kill my kind."

"That's a knife!" cried Frances over the top of Godfrey's complaining.

"So that's what this is called," exclaimed the giant ape, waving the blade. "My father made this one, as the other one became much too small as he grew bigger."

Remembering a television documentary her father had been watching, Mary suddenly gasped. "Wow, wind it back a minute – are you talking about the Bigfoot?"

Up came the giant foot. Inspecting it with careful consideration, Mr Tiggle-Trotter stated, "I don't think my feet are that big. Quite average for a Trotter of my age."

Watching the limb return to the floor, Frances explained, "In America, the native people call you Sasquatch."

"You're both right. Humans know us by both names," answered Mr Tiggle-Totter. "But when my grandfather was little, he went somewhere else in your world, completely different to the forest. He was always off and taking vacation. My father said you just couldn't stop him – no sooner was he back than off he would go again."

Mary's idea of somewhere other than forests was that of a lovely summer holiday abroad, sunning herself on a beach. "Spain's gorgeous this time of year. It's the height of the season at the moment. Did he go somewhere warm?" she asked.

"Mountaineering," replied Mr Tiggle-Trotter fondly. "He was a keen climber in his youth, with many visits to your land."

Mary's dulling eyes showed no interest in the pursuit of climbing. "That could get a little chilly," she shivered.

"Not for a Tiggle-Trotter," he smiled. Then he returned to the telling of his story. "My grandfather would seek out the highest of ranges, and when he discovered the roof of the world – and that's the Himalayan mountains in the region of Nepal and Tibet – he never went anywhere else."

"It gets very cold up there," shuddered Frances Fidget-Knickers.

"Not my kind of holiday, then," insisted Mary Midget-Mouth, with a shiver.

Happily, the giant ape laughed. "But my grandfather loved his climbing and enjoyed it immensely. Unfortunately, after a nasty fall off the summit, and tumbling down and getting covered in snow along the way, he lay in a heap, somewhat dazed for a while."

"Did he hurt himself?" gasped Frances.

"Not at all," smiled Mr Tiggle-Trotter. "We apes are a very hardy bunch."

"What happened next?" asked Mary.

"My grandfather, thinking it was a remote and foreboding land, and mostly uninhabited, got up to brush himself down. The lapse in concentration gave him quite a shock as he stood up, for there was a procession of Tibetan monks staring at him. Startled and surprised, he ran away. Next thing you know, we are being called Yeti. In Tibetan, the word means 'magical creature', which I like more than Abominable Snowman – that sounds so menacing."

"Miss Frances and Miss Mary," said Godfrey, "I think we've got a bit sidetracked."

At the jogging of her mind, Frances gasped, "Oh yes, so we have." Then she asked, "Do you have any knives and forks, then?"

Mr Tiggle-Trotter put down the huge cutting tool and filled his wooden plate, on top of which you could park two cars. "No, use your hands and fingers," he munched, after a haystack of veg hit his plate. "Tuck in – it's an anything-you-like salad."

"In that case," beamed Godfrey, quickly tucking a cloth under his chin, "I think I will have a Christmas turkey dinner."

Giant handfuls of salad were raised up to a giant mouth, and into it went the vegetables. With teeth the size of A4 sheets of paper grinding them down to be swallowed, Mr Tiggle-Trotter mumbled, "Marmalade toasted sandwiches." With a gulp, the food was gone. Then he repeated the shovelling of food. "Peanut jelly crackers," he gulped. After the gulping, a new replacement of vegetables was quickly gobbled up. "Fruit cocktail and cream … simply divine!" he cried.

Godfrey got ready to take his first bite. With a munch and a crunch, he mumbled, "Miss Frances and Miss Mary, give it a try." Then he stopped chewing, as the flavour swished around inside his mouth. "I say, they're the crispest roast potatoes I've had in ages!" he gasped.

An instant thought of pure delight hit Mary Midget-Mouth. "It must be like Mrs-Give-Us-A-Giggle's food drink!" she cried, grabbing at the salad excitedly. In it went with a gobbling chew, and out it came with a spluttering cough. "Broccoli! Yuk, yuk and triple yuk!"

Godfrey nibbled on. "Anything-you-like salad is what it is. And anything you think of will be the taste in your mouth. Miss Mary, try not to let your mind wander." As he finished the words, the rodent was taken by surprise. "My word, a sea food platter – how wonderful!" Now addressing the youngest member of the Knickers family household, he gave some very sound advice. "Miss Frances, why don't you give it a try? Focus, now – it's all in the way you think about it."

As thoughts of unpleasant tastes she had never experienced ran wild, she hesitated. "What if I get it all muddled up? Like belly button fluff and flaky ear wax or smelly armpits?"

Spluttering and coughing, Mary gagged. "Don't go giving me ideas … this is bad enough!"

Mr Tiggle-Trotter put the brakes on his own eating and informed them, "I always think of birthdays, especially my presents – it works wonders for me." He then returned to the clump of veg held in his hand. Teeth tearing at it, he rejoiced. "Flapjacks and honey, with yogurt topping … yum diddle yum yum."

Very slowly, Frances bit into a stick of celery. "Baked beans and strawberry jelly," she said in surprise. "How very odd!"

71

"Miss Frances, I think you're getting your flavours mixed up. Can't you think of anything nice?"

And there it was, thought Frances, coming up with an empty sheet. "I'm struggling to come up with something. Nope, it's a total blank."

"Oh dear," sighed the giant ape, and his mind turned sour along with his mouth. "Rotten cabbage – at least no maggots this time!" he smiled.

Even Mary couldn't think of anything, until she finally had a surprising mouthful of salad. "Apple strudel and custard … that's it … the last time I had that was at Mrs-Give-Us-A-Giggle's shop. Why don't you think of that?"

A few seconds later, they soon settled down into a conversation over the most extraordinary meal.

"Granddad Sprinkle-Tinkle – what a nasty old man," munched the giant ape. Enthusiastically, he gasped. "Wowee, chocolate torsade – get in there!"

The celery stick that Frances Fidget-Knickers was chewing on changed. "Roast beef and Yorkshire puddings," she blinked, staring at the stem. Then she asked her question. "What other beastly things did my rotten grandfather do?"

"Yuk!" exclaimed Mary in disgust. "Boiled cabbage – for a moment there, I was thinking about my father telling me to eat my greens."

Ignoring her, Mr Tiggle-Trotter stated, "Granddad Sprinkle-Tinkle is nothing but a crook and a thief. He swindled retired people out of their life savings, leaving them destitute with nowhere to live." Again, the salad he was munching on changed, and he sighed, "Spaghetti with mozzarella cheese … superb!"

Mouth nibbling, Godfrey agreed. "That he did, the heartless old grump left them on the streets with nothing but the clothes on their backs." With a delicate nibble, he added happily, "Pepperoni pizza, I haven't had that for a while."

With a hesitant bite that took her by surprise, Mary said, "Icing sugar and marzipan … I love almonds. By the way, how many people did he con?"

The giant ape's eyes started to water. "Hundreds, maybe thousands," he gasped. "Chilli peppers – my, that was a hot one."

"Those poor people," munched Frances, as she crunched on a carrot. "Lemon meringue pie – I'd never have guessed that. So did the victims get any of their money back?"

The giant shook his head.

The rodent stopped eating.

Puffing to cool his mouth down, the giant ape answered. "Not one penny. They say he stashed it somewhere, but nobody knows where." His giant hand stuffed a clump of lettuce into his gigantic mouth, and then he smiled. "Mushroom ravioli, delicious."

The anything-you-like salad was causing Mary Midget-Mouth some problems, as her thoughts kept changing. "Spring onions, yuk! A triple burger and ketchup, that's better. Chocolate brownies, yum!" Then her face screwed up in disgust. "Broccoli again – yuk, with icing on the top!"

"Miss Mary, try not to let your mind wander," said Godfrey again, as he was taken by surprise. "Goodness me … it's lemon sherbet ice cream, how delightful!"

Frances said, "If only there was some way of finding the money and giving it all back." Tasting a small morsel of food, which exploded into an amazing, mouth-watering experience, she smiled brightly. "Black forest gateau with chocolate orange twists – wow, how fab was that?"

Mr Tiggle-Trotter stopped his eating. "There might be a way of finding out. I have records of the many court cases the rotten old toad attended."

Godfrey sighed heavily. "I'm not too sure these young ones here should be reading about such terrible events."

"Shocking or not," Frances insisted, "I want to know the truth. All of it, if you please!"

"Ooooh, a bit of family history," Mary said excitedly. "I wonder how much dirt you will dig up."

Godfrey gave the thought inside his head a lot of consideration before he spoke. "It would be nice to see the look on Granddad Sprinkle-Tinkle's face. Especially if we managed to find out where all the money has been stashed. Then we could return it to its rightful owners."

After their meal, they left the room to research the documentation.

CHAPTER 9

THE LIBRARY

Frances, Mary and Godfrey were carried by the giant ape through a labyrinth of passageways. Again, the sound of wildlife filled the air as he walked through the maze. Slowly, as they went on, the sounds of birds and insects gradually faded, as they approached an ordinary looking door. On it were the words: "BOOKS READING – QUIET, PLEASE".

That's odd, thought Frances. *Shouldn't the sign say "book-reading" instead of "books"?*

"Quietly now," hushed Mr Tiggle-Trotter.

"Miss Frances and Miss Mary," whispered Godfrey, "best behaviour please."

In they went.

What a truly magnificent room it was, with row after row of shelves stacked full of novels. The library was three times taller than the giant ape, with a dome-top ceiling made of glass. Through the panes the sunlight glistened down, filling the magnificent room with light. Stacks and stacks of thousands of all sorts of books were wall to wall, floor to ceiling, and in every available space.

There was a hint of murmuring noises, as though a lot of people were reading under their breath. "We have some guests," announced Mr Tiggle-Trotter. "Please behave."

A voice came back – and just a voice. It echoed out, "Quiet, please."

The murmuring stopped, as the person belonging to the voice slid around one of the bookshelves. It gestured to the room. "Thank you for your cooperation."

It was an unexpected sight, as the whatever-it-was slithered forwards.

It wasn't human, with its long body flowing into a long, thin head. On top sat the thickest of lensed glasses. The glass lenses magnified its eyes, which looked out of place on a figure about the same size as Godfrey.

"Hello there, Miss Read-It, and how are you keeping? Been up to much today?" asked Godfrey.

"Just reading. Who are they?" huffed Miss Read-It, peering at the two girls. "I'll have you know I keep a well-run library here. No nonsense, if you know what I mean."

"Forgive me, where are my manners? This is Miss Frances and Miss Mary," Godfrey smiled, gesturing to show Miss Read-It who was who.

"How do you do?" sniffed the whatever-it-was most politely.

Frances and Mary were quite glad they were standing on the giant ape's hand, out of harm's way. They were unsure whether Miss Read-It might be a venomous creature.

"Are you a snake?" asked Frances.

Mary butted in before Miss Read-it could answer. "You're not poisonous, are you?"

Miss Read-It wriggled disapprovingly. "I'm most certainly not a cold-blooded reptile," she insisted, with a shudder. And then she wriggled importantly. "I'm a worm, and a very well-read bookworm at that."

Moving closer to Miss Read-It, the giant ape took a step forwards and said, "We are looking for Granddad Sprinkle-Tinkle's case files."

The look on the bookworm's face was that of shock. "Keep your voice down," she hushed in a startled tone, "or there will be an almighty fuss."

Mary, not fully understanding Miss Read-It's concern, called out, "But it's just some old books you've got stored somewhere!"

Suddenly there was a rustling of paper, followed by a supersonic boom of disapproving noise. The cries of thousands of disgruntled novels were protesting extremely loudly.

"Stored away?"

"Never to be read, perish the thought!"

"Old books, who's calling us old?"

"Now you've gone and done it," sighed Miss Read-It, unhappily. "It will take me ages to settle them all back down again."

Mr Tiggle-Trotter stamped his enormous foot. "That will be enough of that, if you don't mind. I will not tolerate bad behaviour. You should be ashamed of yourselves – is that any way to behave in front of our guests?"

The books sulked and said nothing.

"Mr Tiggle Trotter," gasped Frances, joyfully. "You have talking books – how simply delightful! Books are my most favourite things in the whole world."

Hearing this, the novels started again like a flock of seagulls at feeding time, fighting over the scraps.

"Pick me!"

"No, not that one, me!"

"Me, me, me, pick me!"

Miss Read-It wormed herself in and out of the shelves, worried. "What with guests and all the commotion, now they're excited. Not sure how I'm going to shut them up."

"Silence!" cried the giant ape. "Any more of that and you will be packed away!"

Instantly, not a sound was heard.

Godfrey gulped. "Oh my, that's very harsh."

"Is it?" asked Mary.

With a shiver, Miss Read-It stiffened. "Books like to be read, not ignored," she answered.

"What could be worse than not reading a book?" asked Mary.

"Not having any in the first place," shuddered the bookworm. "I'd be out of a job."

"That is a shocking thought," agreed Godfrey. "But not as upsetting as the criminal activities Granddad Sprinkle-Tinkle got up to."

"Miss Read-It," said Mr Tiggle-Trotter, "could you please get the case files?"

Turning and worming away, she wriggled forwards and out of sight. From behind a stack of shelves they heard her mutter, "I put them in the section of the library marked 'extremely dangerous'."

On the hearing of this, the books delivered their message for all to hear.

"Danger, danger, don't trust a stranger. Crimes of shock and awe, make for the door. Cash and stash for a rainy day. Over the sands of red and far away. Look for a lock without a door."

Watching Miss Read-It struggle back with the biggest book she had ever seen, Mary asked, "What does that all mean?"

"I have no idea," answered Frances, as Miss Read-It disappeared around one of the bookcases.

"Danger, don't trust a stranger," muttered Mary, watching the bookworm return with another cumbersome manual.

"Crimes and door," puzzled Frances, as Miss Read-It disappeared again.

"Cash and stash," mumbled Mary, as another bound hardback was brought out and put with the others.

"Sands of red," quizzed Frances, just catching Miss Read-It turning out of sight.

"Lock without a door. What lock has no door?" asked Mary.

"Miss Frances and Miss Mary, it's puzzling, that's for sure," Godfrey said, watching the pile of documents grow. "Every time we decide to look at the case files, the books repeat the same old message over and over again."

The bookworm panted and puffed as she dropped the last of the journals. "Twenty-two in all, and thank goodness I don't have them all. The rest of them are stored in the Court of Appeal."

Mary looked down at her hands and remembered a snide remark that Granddad Sprinkle-Tinkle had made to her earlier that day. "I don't think he's very appealing. When he gave me the scissors to cut the grass this morning, he said that if I didn't stop biting my fingernails, he would pull them out."

Rubbing her eyes with concentration, Frances said, "My mum and dad don't seem to notice how horrid he is."

Godfrey pondered before he spoke. "If no one is noticing the awful and wicked ways of Granddad Sprinkle-Tinkle, I'm wondering if he's smuggled some sort of magic back with him."

The giant ape answered, as he put all three of them down. "It's possible, but it would need to be the darkest of magic spells."

With his silver-topped cane held tight underarm, the rodent marched forwards. "How very sneaky – let's see what else he has got up to."

Miss Read-It placed a book on the Victorian mahogany reading table, with its elegantly carved leg taking the weight and spreading out at the bottom into four fingers. She opened the journal. "Sorry, you're far too young to be hearing about that kind of thing," she insisted. With a snap, it was closed, and very quickly replaced with another book. "Here we are," she shivered, "this will do … it makes for some grim reading, though."

Frances and Mary ran over to Miss Read-It.

Mary got there first. "How do you read that? It's just a lot of pictures of funny-looking animals and people!"

"So it is," said Frances, as she caught up. "Looks like hieroglyphics."

Mary shrugged slightly. "Okay – don't tell me you know what it means?"

Frances answered her friend. "I know what it is, but not how to read it."

The giant ape's eyes focused on the bookworm. "I struggle terribly with reading this language – do you know how to read hieroglyphics, Miss Read-It?"

"Of course," she replied. "One of my great loves is ancient Egypt. On the other hand, the weather is blisteringly hot and not suited to us worms. Out there, I would shrivel up in no time from the heat of the sun."

Mr Tiggle-Trotter smiled and asked politely, "Would you mind reading it for us?"

Agreeing, and thoroughly inspecting the pages, she muttered, "Not much here, just a lot of legal jargon." The pages kept turning as she mumbled from time to time. "Really, people do that sort of thing?" Still she continued to read until all of a sudden she announced formally, "Here it is. This is what you are looking for."

Like a ghostly character, Mary asked in a spooky voice, "Skeletons in the closet – what does it say?"

Miss Read-It inspected the official records with great interest before saying, "Does she need a doctor?" No one answered, so she read to herself and gasped, "Do you know, I think there's been a mix up! These are the uncensored court documents."

"What does that mean?" asked Frances.

Uneasily, Godfrey stepped forwards. "Miss Frances, these are the original files that Granddad Sprinkle-Tinkle tried to hide. Somehow they have ended up here by mistake."

The bookworm wriggled and cleared her throat. "It makes for some awful reading. It might be better to skip this section."

Mr Tiggle-Trotter stood tall and proudly said, "I don't think that would be acceptable after nearly being killed today. Miss Frances is entitled to an explanation at the very least. After all, she did save all our lives."

There was no disagreement from Miss Read-It, as the official document was read. "On the counts of kidnapping children to sell into slavery, all six hundred and seventy-eight were found to be true."

"He didn't?" gasped Frances.

"He did," gulped Godfrey.

Expressing her concern, Frances Fidget-Knickers sighed, "Those poor children – where are they now?"

"No one knows," answered the giant ape with a heavy breath.

"Does it not say in the files?" asked Mary.

The bookworm peered deep into the pages and read some more. "By means of pretending to be able to find the stolen children, he fiddled money out of his victims."

"That's low, very low," Frances said, her voice changing. "What a nasty, horrid man he is!"

"How mean is that?" added Mary, looking angry.

Miss Read-It carried on. "It states here that Granddad Sprinkle-Tinkle made lots of trips across the Desert of Death by a Thousand Huts."

"Don't you mean cuts?" asked Frances.

"No, it states huts quite clearly here," answered the bookworm, re-reading the page.

"That's not good news," revealed Mr Tiggle-Trotter, going on, "The Mirage People live in those huts. They pull you in with illusions of all your favourite things. Once they have you, there is no going back. Death soon follows."

Unexpectedly, the book shelves started to rattle and the novels started to say, "Danger, danger, don't trust a stranger."

"That's it!" cried Frances, her detective thoughts bubbling out.

"Is it, Miss Frances?" asked Godfrey.

Excitedly, Frances Fidget-Knickers said, "Don't you get it? The stranger is my grandfather!"

The books started to speak again. "Shock and awe, we said make for the door."

"Have you figured it out?" spluttered Mary.

"Almost," Frances smiled. "The crimes of kidnapping children are shock and awe. Make for the door is when he came back to ask for money."

The books spoke again. "Cash and stash, we said for a rainy day."

Pleased with herself, Frances blurted out, "It's hidden somewhere dry and safe."

Delightedly, Mr Tiggle-Trotter smiled. "I think we are onto something."

"I quite agree," acknowledged Godfrey.

Frances asked for quiet as the books spoke again. "Over the sands of red and far away, we told you."

"Sands that are red," muttered Frances, before asking, "Does the Desert of Death have red sands?"

"Why yes, Miss Frances."

"I bet it's far away?" asked Mary.

"That it is, Miss Mary."

With the last part of the riddle, the books spoke again. "Look for a lock, we said, without a door." With that, they fell silent.

Thoughtfully, Frances mumbled, "I'm not getting that last bit." Then she froze and went into deep thought, as her truly remarkable brain worked on solving the problem.

"Here we go," said Mary Midget-Mouth. "I've seen this before. She's working it all out in her head. We won't get much out of Frances until she either works out the problem or gives up trying."

They all looked at her as she muttered, "A lock and no door … a key … but no door … what could that mean? A door and no lock … what has a door but no lock?" There were a few moments of silence after the last words were spoken. Then her eyes marvelled brilliantly. "Does the Desert of Death have water anywhere?" she asked.

Mr Tiggle Trotter thought carefully. "To the east is a lake," he replied.

"That's it!" cried Frances, excitedly. "Don't you see? That's where he's hidden the money!"

"Is it?" puzzled Mary, questioningly.

With a beaming smile, Frances informed them, "Just like Loch Ness in Scotland, it's a strip of water. And lochs don't have doors."

"There are caves scattered around the body of water," said the great ape. "Some are too small for me to enter."

Godfrey jumped for joy. "By Jove, she's only gone and solved the riddle!" he cried.

Mr Tiggle-Trotter suddenly froze; his giant ears twitched, as faint scratching noises made their way through the air. "Someone is at the front door."

The stranger waiting outside was about to change everything for them all.

CHAPTER 10

THE RAT

The front door was opened. A rag-tag figure lay before them, collapsed from exhaustion. The rat had keeled over from the sheer effort of finding the giant primate's home. Around both ankles were bare patches of skin. Eyes closed, holding a letter tightly to his chest with both hands, he looked almost dead.

"Quick, put me down," urged Frances, shaking the magic box.

As soon as she was at the rat's side, a black animal with a white streak running down its back appeared from the box. "Stand back," advised the voice of Mrs Give-Us-A-Giggle. "Give the little darling some room to work!"

Mary panicked. "It's a skunk!"

"How clever of you, me dear," replied the voice of Mrs Give-Us-A-Giggle. "This one won't hurt you. Remember, Frances, you'll need to give it instructions." And then the voice was gone.

Frances spoke to the creature. "The poor thing is in need of your help – please don't let it die."

Turning its back, the skunk squirted a small amount of liquid and swished its bushy tale to spread the odour. As everybody caught the scent, the sweet smell of all their most favourite memories came flooding back.

Its fragrance jogged the giant ape's mind, as the pheromones brought out a sigh with the memories. "My mother – such lovely cuddles."

Godfrey smiled. "Nickley Woods, the place where I was born."

As the essence of wet dog hit Mary, she laughed fondly, "Oh Millie, you and your bath times … you little rascal!"

For Frances, it was different; the only nice memories she had were those of her dad's extremely hot spices and the tricks she had played on her nasty grandfather. "Well done, me," she said, pleased with herself.

Now the perfumed incense did what it was supposed to do. The exhausted rat opened his eyes very slowly. He muttered and mumbled. Then he coughed and spluttered out some words, confused. "Is that you … please don't take me back … you're hurting me!"

With its work done, the skunk disappeared before their eyes, while Frances, Mary and Godfrey attended to the injured stranger. "It's okay, you're safe now," smiled his fellow rodent, reassuringly.

"What … where am I?" asked the dazed rat, clutching the letter very tightly. "You're not Mr Tiggle-Trotter?" All three of them moved so the visitor could see the giant ape. "Ha, there you are – he said you would be big. It's very important you get this."

"First things first," hushed the giant ape. "You're in need of medical attention."

Hurrying, all three, along with the frail-looking rodent, were taken into the hand of the giant ape. Quickly, he ran to a room that smelt of surgical spirits and medicines. "Mr Hack-It, we have a medical emergency!" he cried.

The rat panicked and his lips drew back, exposing the little fellow's large incisors. "Please, whatever you do, don't amputate my tail!"

Godfrey, as someone else from the gnawing mammal family, understood the concerns of the frightened traveller. "There, there, my dear chap, your tail's in fine form." Checking the rest of the rat, he asked, "Whatever happened to the fur on your legs?"

"Shackles," answered the weary rodent. "I was taken when I was just a pup and thrown into slavery by the Snogg-Snifflers."

"That's dreadful," gasped Frances.

"Not really," said the rat. "Being young saved my life. No meat, you see – not enough on my bones to worry about. Instead, I was put in chains to keep house and tidy up after them. I can't complain much, as it's better than the cooking pot." With a frightful look, he sliced his hand across his throat and gurgled. "If you know what I mean."

"Well, you won't get any of that sort of thing here," insisted Mary sternly. "Not if Mr Tiggle-Trotter has anything to say about it."

The rodent's eyes were soulless from the many years in servitude. His spirit had been beaten out of him, whipped away by the savage floggings. Holding out the letter, he spoke. "Mr Tiggle-Trotter, I promised I would get this to you." Slowly, his limbs went limp and he lay perfectly still.

"Is he dead?" asked Mary.

The rodent's left eye opened and he sighed. "No, but at least half of me is resting. You can take the letter."

"It can wait – let's see to you first," insisted the giant ape, taking the envelope. "I'll just put it over here." With a shout, the primate cried again, "Doctor of the house, we need some help!"

A mummy came in, and he was nothing like how you might expect a medical person to look. Covered in bandages, he whinged just like a certain assistant at Mrs Give-Us-A-Giggle's joke shop. "As if I haven't got enough to do, now I'm being shouted at. It's not fair. Out of order and unprofessional, that's what it is." Addressing them all, he moaned on. "We doctors get very little sleep. Always on call for this and that, and the awkward others. Okay,

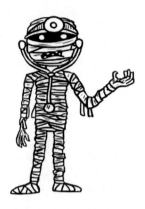

whatever, whatever, whatever seems to be the problem now?"

"Here we go," smirked Mary, thinking back to the mummified shop assistant. "Mr Whinge-Pot, doing a bit of moonlighting, are we?"

"Really? Is it you, Mr Whinge-Pot?" asked Frances.

The doctor examined the situation. "Nasty, very nasty," he said, breathing out slowly. "The rat I can help. As for those two asking for a Mr Whinge-Pot, I think they've gone mad. I could always ask the professor's assistant, Mr Gone-Bonkers, to take a look at them, if you like?"

"Miss Frances and Miss Mary, this is not Mr Whinge-Pot," stated Godfrey, referring to the mummy. "This is Mr Hack-It; he is a doctor of great standing in the community."

Moaning and whinging, Mr Hack-It said, "Why did I bother? Seven years studying at the university to be a pathologist, only to get mistaken for someone else. I've only been struck off five times, and none of the names I used were Mr Whinge-Pot."

"See, what did I tell you? He comes highly recommended," beamed Godfrey, watching his fellow rodent climb onto an examination table.

The patient's arm was tugged very hard by Mr Hack-It. "Does that hurt?"

"Ouch!" cried the rodent.

"Should he be doing that?" asked Mary.

"I don't think so," answered Frances.

Mr Hack-it poked and prodded at the rat's body. "How about that – feel any discomfort?"

"Ouch, ouch, ouch!" cried the rodent with each poke.

"Splendid!" cried Mr Hack-It. "The nervous system seems to be working perfectly!"

"I'm not surprised," shuddered Mary. "If you were poking me like that, I'd be jumping all over the place."

Analysing the rodent a little more, Mr Hack-It asked, "Can you open your mouth and stick your tongue out?"

The rat swallowed with discomfort, and then he did exactly what he was asked. A large pair of surgical pliers gripped the mobile mass of tissue.

The rodent flinched.

"That looks uncomfortable," shuddered Frances.

"Brace yourself," smiled Mr Hack-It.

"Okay," gurgled the rat.

The tongue was given a very hard pull.

Eyes watering, the rodent winced in pain. "Aghhh!"

"Splendid response," beamed Mr Hack-It, "and I never had to ask you to say a thing."

Almost without thinking, the giant ape muttered, "Interesting work – when you normally do that, they don't say anything."

"I know – this is the first time it's happened!" cried Mr Hack-It. "My patients are normally dead when I make my examinations!"

As the penny dropped, Frances Fidget-Knickers said, "Just a minute – pathologists perform autopsies?"

"That we do, and I've never had a complaint yet from any of mine," declared Mr Hack-It, letting the tongue go. "Wish I could say the same for the relatives."

The rat got up and dusted himself down. "You'll get none out of me. I'm extremely grateful for your assistance."

"See?" smiled Godfrey, revealing his admiration. "What a marvel to medical science. A top-notch doctor if ever I saw one."

"Thanks for fixing me up, Doc," said the rodent, turning his attention towards the giant primate. "How about we open that letter now?"

CHAPTER 11

A LETTER

The letter was opened. A huge projection light shone out. Like a drive-in cinema, the story unfolded before them.

"I is the King," grunted a hog, standing next to Granddad Sprinkle-Tinkle, "and I is having a mind-changing decision."

All the boars were assembled before his majesty in the great hall, with one of them asking, "Is you? What does you be deciding, Your Splendidness?"

"I is not waiting anymore," snorted the royal one, through flared nostrils. "We is off to farms today, and Him is leading the way."

"You is?" came the awkward question.

With his royal mood showing no tolerance, he roared out, "No I is not, I does not know the way. Him is showing us, isn't you, Granddad Sprinkle-Tinkle?"

The useless excuse for a grandfather, with his wicked grin, complained, "I hope I'm not getting carried again, especially the way I was brought here. Very uncomfortable – I might have a lapse in concentration and forget where to go."

"You is not worry your brainy head about that," grinned the ruler of the Snogg-Snifflers. "We is travelling together in my royal carriage."

The horrid old man sniffed. With an arrogant air of snootiness, he grumbled, "I suppose I could give it a try – it's got to be better than slumming it."

"We is not elevating lower classes of Snifflers to royal way of travel," insisted the King. "They is lower ranks and belonging in Run-It-Class."

On hearing this, one of the rugged brutes declared, "Only superior officers – and our crowned-headed one is bums-on-seat way of travelling."

Without a care in the world, their monarch stood proud, with the last remaining food stuffs being picked from his teeth. In between the picking and licking, he shouted, "We is all leaving in a few hours, and you is all getting ready faster than tooting-sweet! Any stragglers and I is off chopping your heads and having bacon for my supper tonight!"

No one moved.

No one made a sound.

There was an uneasy silence in the great hall, as his highness snorted with contempt.

He hit the royal chair.

He paused for a moment.

Then he hit the chair again.

And then he boomed, "Well, what is you waiting for? Is you wanting a bit of head-chopping?"

Pandemonium broke out.

"I is not upsetting the King!" cried a horrified Snogg-Sniffler. "My wife has only just started speaking to me again! I is not wanting any more home-troubling if I has no head to answer her with!"

"I is knowing what you is meaning," panicked a beast next to him. "I is still in the dog house from my tongue-tying orders."

"Hanging on some minutes," slobbered a stupid brute. "Why is dogs getting a home when I has only a cardboard box to live in?"

No one answered, as the panicked disorder was watched with great glee by the king of the Snogg-Snifflers. "I does like brawn! Jellied with trotters and tails is best! Faster you is getting to it! Or you is chop, chop for the cooking pot!" he bellowed.

"Your Great One," cried a snotty nosed hog, "we is trying fast as we can!"

The King boomed at the mucus-covered porker. "I is cooking you faster than you is trying!" he barked.

Hopping from one trotter to the other, the beast ran off as the hullabaloo intensified. In the mayhem, Snifflers got turned and twisted around until some of them were facing the wrong way. The way out wasn't big enough for them all, as some of them got stuck. Now wedged like a cork in a bottle, the doorway was jammed full of Snogg-Sniffler bodies. With their arms and legs kicking, and their large frames wriggling, they tried to get free. In their frustration, cries of panic took over.

"I is stuck quicker than gluing!"

"You is not the only one clogged!"

"I is wiggling like worm on a hook, and I is still sticking fast!"

"You is getting your leg out of my mouth or I is having hoof for third afternoon snacking."

Some of the porkers stopped struggling as one of them said, "I is stuck here, and it be time for snacks already."

Then he went on to bite the Snogg-Sniffler next to him.

"Ouch! I is not being a snack to be eaten by you!" moaned the bitten hog, looking for some assistance. "You, over there – you is giving us a push, and we is getting out of this mess faster than quick."

At those instructions, his dim-witted Snogg-Sniffler neighbour gave an almighty push.

Nothing happened.

He ran back a few paces. He picked his spot.

Charging forwards, he hit the wall of porkers.

"Thud" went the sound.

"Twang" went the idiot bouncing off the other Snogg-Snifflers.

Clearly not having learned from the unsuccessful attempt, he decided to run back a few more steps than before and charged at them at full sprinting, speed.

"Crack" went the sound as he hit the wall of bodies.

"Twang" flew the dimwit, bouncing off and landing halfway through the great hall on top of several beasts.

"We is having none of that," snorted one of the Snifflers who had just been hit. "We is picking you up and using you as a battering ram."

"I is thanking you for your help," sighed the very dazed Snogg-Sniffler.

The King of the Hogs eagerly shouted, "You is putting your backs into it." Turning to Granddad Sprinkle-Tinkle, he snorted, "Military training and problem-solving this be."

With some doubt, the old man replied, "You don't say."

"Character-building," sniffed the King, with great interest. "Makes a Sniffler of you, it does." Then he commanded, "Ramming speed you is doing now!"

Seven Snogg-Snifflers picked up the bewildered hog. Three each side and one from behind, they charged with all their strength, smashing through the wall of stuck bodies.

Tumbling like skittles, the Snogg-Snifflers went bouncing like wooden pins down the entrance to the great hall.

His royal highness smiled with admiration. "What is I telling you? They is highly trained – problem solved. We is being on our way in a couple of hours …"

The letter started to flicker and fade.

"That's not good news," sighed Mr Tiggle-Trotter, folding the piece of paper. "What are we going to do about it?"

"There's more," said the threadbare rodent. "A rat lost his life getting that letter to me. I'm not sure who wrote the rest, but it was shoved in my hand as a Snogg-Sniffler unshackled me. As soon as I was free, I legged it. My fellow pals were not so lucky."

Once again, the letter was opened and the magical movement of unbelievable images began.

This time the Snogg-Snifflers were somewhere different, as the letter began its words and motion.

"Faster!" shouted a brute, cracking down a leather whip and lashing one of the chained rats. The small mammal winced in pain as the whip hit his back with its stinging kiss. "You is pulling royal carriage faster. You is putting your backs into it or I is sting-whipping you again."

A line of one hundred rats, fifty to each side, were shackled to the carriage. Behind them were more wagons, with rodents pulling them like workhorses. The army marched into the canyon and halted before the commanding Snogg-Sniffler.

"Looks like we is here," smiled the King. "Has you ever tasted ape before?"

"I can't say that I have," answered the old bag of bones. "Is it like chicken? I quite like the legs, myself."

Opening the carriage door, the King got up and stepped out with a laugh. "You is finding out all for yourself soon enough."

Granddad Sprinkle-Tinkle followed his royal highness. "I'd like a bit of parsley with mine," he sniggered.

The commanding Snogg-Sniffler stood trembling along with the second in command. They dared not speak, as they greeted their mighty one with a bow.

"Raaaa, we is at our outpost," commented the King, flexing his body and stretching his limbs.

Still bent over, the two beasts kept their heads very low.

With a slap on Granddad Sprinkle-Tinkle's back, the royal one announced, "This is being where we is getting new supplies. Then we is refreshed and off to pillage farms."

The leech of an old man sniggered some more. "Wonderful, I'm looking forward to topping up me wealth. I wonder how much money they've got stashed away."

With a belly button wiggle, the King sniffed his finger and sneezed. "That does clear my hooter." Through watering eyes, he greeted the two trembling hogs. "Ups you is looking."

The second in command tried to save his skin by spluttering out, "I is not the one. I is only following orders. He is the ordering and making boo-boo. I is not dumpling-head like him."

"What?" grunted the King to the commander. "You is explaining yourself fast and quick."

Quivering, the commander stammered, "We is trying very hard, but they has magic box. Powerful spell-making it be, and Tiggle-Trotter is getting away. I is not wanting punishments. You is being merciful king."

There was no sound from the monarch, as his head started to turn a different colour from anger.

"Now you is doing it," cringed the lower-ranking officer. "Looks like we is in for the Word!"

With cries that the Word might be said, every Snogg-Sniffler who had been sent to ambush the giant primate ran for cover.

"The Word!" yelped a hog.

"Not the dreaded Word," whimpered another Snogg-Sniffler.

With his eyes fixed on the King, a snout-cowering beast squirmed. "He is going to say it."

By this time, their monarch's head was steaming with rage.

The temper sparked inside his skull and crackled like crazy, and with it little puffs of steam shot out of his ears.

Now fully charged, the King jumped up and down on the spot, and let fly with the Word. "I is upniod!!!" he boomed.

The force from the bellowing monarch nearly blew over the commanding Snogg-Sniffler.

"See?" said the second in command. "You is upsetting and annoying our king all at the same time. You is a bad leader."

Two hundred and forty-nine troops who had upset their monarch began their fearful fidgeting.

Some looked left. Some looked right. All of them turned their attention to their royal one to see what he would say.

As if with thunderbolts of lightning, the King kept bellowing, "You is incompetent nincompoop! You is useless excuse for a commander! You is dysfunctional at best! Worthless bit of slime you is and fruitless with your task!" The King stopped. Eyes flashing as though a volcano had exploded inside his head, he screamed, "You is idle, no-good hog and you Snifflers under his command are no better! Upniod, upniod, upniod!"

Hearing this, there was panic in the Snogg-Sniffler ranks. Defensive protests started.

"We is only following useless one's orders."

"Idle hog is useless at giving them."

"Nincompoop is to blame for no fruits."

The commanding Snogg-Sniffler dropped to his knees and pleaded, "I is begging your forgiveness. I is liking my body in one piece."

With disgust, the King snorted, "Relations!"

With a turning of the screws, the commander whispered to the King, "What would my sister say? She is your wife, and she is not being too happy if I is getting the chop!"

The king of the Snogg-Snifflers exchanged uneasy looks as he whispered back, "She is formidable foe, and she is making my life woefully miserable if you is dead." At that, an idea flashed into his head that would save him from a very unhappy wife. "You is listening quick and I is making jargon and you is saying something good about me?"

"I is doing that, Your Kingship," agreed the monarch's relative.

Throwing the commander to one side, the King made his speech. "I is not just blaming one Sniffler for this mess we is now in. You is all a bunch of morons, and you is all responsible."

The commander acted quickly and leered at his troops. "Our sovereign is hitting nail on the head with your slapdash ways. You is all slipshod with your shoddiness," he grunted.

"You is right," agreed the King. "I is thinking now you is not smashing Tiggle-Trotter over the bonce, we is all going hungry because you is all useless. I is thinking you is all making up for the lack of food." The King then gave his royal instruction. "Get out the cooking pot!"

There were gulps of dismay. There were cries of mercy, as the thought of being chopped up dawned on the hogs.

"I has a family; you is showing clemency, oh Great One!"

"I is asking for leniency, I is having kiddy-winks at home!"

"Amnesty – I is asking for reprieve, Your Royalness!"

The monarch continued his ruse. "Why is I sparing you when we is having empty bellies?"

A speaker for the soon-to-be-executed hogs spoke up. "We is doing anything to save our hides," he grovelled.

"Anything – is you sure of that?" the King replied with a smile.

Nervously, they all glanced at their monarch. Out came a reply. "We is."

"Well, then," grunted the King, "you is all pulling the wagons and my royal carriage."

"What?" gasped the speaker for the hogs. In surprise, he snorted, "And what is all the rats doing?"

The King gave his best performance and cast his eyes over the cooking pot being dragged his way. "They is going in the cauldron for supper tonight, because you lot is their pulling replacements."

There came an almighty cheering from the army of grateful Snogg-Snifflers, as a celebration of fights broke out. Thwack, whack and smack went the blows, until a Snogg-Sniffler said, "Why is we not doing this to rats?"

They all stopped. They all agreed. And the culling began.

As the pile of rodent bodies kept growing, a fat, repulsive beast shuffled forwards. "You is wanting me, Your Wonderfulness?"

"When does you think dinner is ready?" asked the King. "Because I is liking rodents a little sour. Rancid is best, me is thinking."

The cook shuffled over to the dead rats and patted the corpses. "We is coming into the warmest bit of day. If we is leaving them here, we is having the sun making them mouldy, musty, reeking smelly. Whiffy putrid, they is ending up, and you is getting nice, putrefied supper."

A shout roared out. "One is getting away!"

Then the letter ended.

"That's you escaping?" Frances asked the weary rat.

"I was the only one to escape," he replied, pained.

Mr Tiggle-Trotter asked his question to the rodent. "How long will it take them to get to the farms?"

"A day and a half – maybe two at the most," he answered. "I'm not sure if I'm up to much in the way of helping, but I'll give it my best shot!"

"My dear chap," smiled the giant ape, "you've done more than enough already." Starting to search, Mr Tiggle-Trotter stressed, "I'm afraid we have no time to waste. We've got an army to make. Has anyone seen my book on origami?"

CHAPTER 12

THE ORIGAMI ARMY

The escaped rodent, with his new-found freedom, stayed with Mr Hack-It in the medical wing, and the rest of them now found themselves in the arts and crafts room, filled with odds and ends.

The giant ape, with all three in one hand, was still looking for the book on paper folding. "Where did I put it?" he questioned himself. "Maybe it's up there?" He looked to his hand and asked them all, "Do you mind taking a look?"

Before Frances, Mary and Godfrey could answer, a giant arm went up like an elevator. It was a few moments before they stopped just short of the ceiling. "Do you see it?" he asked.

"Sorry, it's not up here," answered Godfrey.

The elevated arm came down faster than it went up, and the sudden empty-stomach feeling of a fairground ride hit them.

"Blimey," gasped Frances, "I wasn't expecting that."

Eagerly, Mary screamed with joy, "Don't you just love it when that happens? Please can we do it again?

Godfrey rearranged himself. Stroking his whiskers, he wobbled, "That will do, thank you very much. Once is quite enough, Miss Mary."

Frances Fidget-Knickers' attention had turned to the many odd things dotted around the place, and the strange ways in which they moved. The "heads" on people-shaped bunting would turn from side to side. Decorated candles would light up and then go out again. Mobiles of horses

hung from the ceiling. They ran around in circles, jumping make-believe fences.

On the table, clay modelling figures dressed in period costumes acted out their pretend dramas.

"Wow, look at all this!" gasped Mary, as all three were put down on the table. "This is way better than Mrs Collage's classroom!"

Over her surprise, Mr Tiggle-Trotter muttered, "Where is it, where is it … perhaps the housekeeper would know."

The performing band of clay models stomped on the table, and one of them stepped forwards. In silence, the acting game was played out.

Watching the figure hold out one hand, Frances Fidget-Knickers asked, "What's it doing?"

"Charades!" cried Mary, enthusiastically. "It's a film?"

A thumbs-down was shown by the clay figure as it went on to put both hands together. Opening them out, palms up, it gestured in silence.

"It's a book," said Frances, recognising the symbol.

Godfrey spluttered excitedly. "Perhaps they are trying to tell us something. Oh, I do like this game, it's so much fun." Then he went on to ask, "Is it a play?"

All the figures shook their heads.

"Just a book, then?" asked the giant ape, seating himself before the table.

The figures nodded. Then one of them put up one finger.

"First word," said Mary. "I'm not very good with book titles."

"Not to worry, Miss Mary," smiled Godfrey, "We have Mr Tiggle-Trotter and Miss Frances on our team."

Now the clay figures worked at assembling some posts. They were erected. They looked like the ones they use in rugby or American football.

"It's something to do with sports?" asked Mary, jumping the gun.

The figures shook their heads. In disagreement, all but one went under the goal post, gesturing the word they were acting.

Enthusiastic guesses came spurting out thick and fast.

"Through?"

"No, going through?"

"Walking through?"

With the main figure shaking its head, the rest of the figures painted a couple of clouds and a jagged bolt of lightning. Then it pointed to the picture while tugging its ears.

Guessing, Mary said, "Is it a storm?"

No, shook the heads of the clay figures.

"Not a storm," muttered Godfrey, studying the picture. "What about a thunderbolt?"

With arms outstretched, the clay figure halted everyone. Shaking its head and clasping an ear, the little actor tugged it.

Mr Tiggle-Trotter mumbled, "Sounds like thunderbolt, but not storm … storm and thunder, makes big noises … is it thunder?"

They shook their heads.

104

"'Under' sounds like 'thunder'," said Frances. "You were going under the goal. The word is under?"

All the clay figures danced with joy as Frances Fidget-Knickers smiled back at them. One of the clay actors put up a hand in a straight line pointing to his chin. Over it he placed the other, so it balanced in the middle.

"That's the letter T!" cried Mary. "It stands for the word 'the'!"

Congratulatory clapping broke out from the clay figures.

"Under the … something," puzzled Godfrey.

Continuing, the sculpted figures put together an armchair and pointed to it as one of them sat down.

"Chair?" asked Mary Midget-Mouth, on a roll.

Uplifting jumps for joy and tumbling acrobatic feats were performed by the happy clay figures, as the last word had been guessed.

"Under the chair," puzzled Frances Fidget-Knickers. "I've never heard of that book.

"Neither have I," pondered Godfrey.

"Don't look at me," sighed Mary with a shrug.

Mr Tiggle-Trotter sat back, and the seat creaked with a thought-jogging noise. "Oops ," he laughed, slightly embarrassed. Then he looked under the chair he was sitting on and spoke sheepishly. "I do believe I've just found it."

After clearing the table, everyone watched the giant ape. The book was opened. "Military personnel and their armaments," he muttered, turning to the right page. "Here it is. Let's see how we do this, then."

Mary had some ideas of her own, and excitedly they came out. "How about some tanks and canons … fighter jets are good, too?" Taking a short breath, she went on. "What about an Apache attack helicopter?"

Immediately, Frances cried, "It could hover in all the awkward spots and shoot down those nasty Snogg-Snifflers!"

"Miss Frances and Miss Mary," said Godfrey, coughing before he spoke again. "I think you are a little overexcited, and you are forgetting that Mr Tiggle-Trotter does not kill any living thing."

"So what's he going to make?" asked Mary.

The giant ape wiggled his finger over the page and declared, "A terracotta army, made from paper."

"You'll need a lot of paper for that," Frances replied. "The Terracotta Army are sculptures depicting the armies of Qin Shi Huang."

"Who?" asked Mary, straight faced and bewildered.

"He was the first emperor of China," answered Frances Fidget-Knickers. "The purpose of the armies he had made was to protect him in the afterlife."

Godfrey looked pleased and smiled, "Well done, Miss Frances. Is there anything else you know about these armies?"

Mary just stood and waited for the reply, as Frances went on in more detail. "According to their roles, the figures vary in height, with the tallest being the generals. The army includes warriors, chariots and horses. Other figures were found, but they were court officials and acrobats and strongmen and musicians. According to the book I read, it took seven-hundred thousand people many years to make them all."

Mary let go her thought. "But we've only got two days at the most, and that includes getting to wherever we are going. How are we going to make everything we need in time?"

The task in front of them was a truly daunting one. Everyone fell silent.

All of them now had blank faces.

Suddenly, there was a whistle from one of the clay figures. Holding their ears, the other sculpted actors came forwards with their offers of help.

"Volunteers!" cried Godfrey. "Good for you – we'd be delighted to have you help us!"

Frances made a quick head count and sighed. "Twenty-four, including us. I don't think that is going to be enough to get the job done in time."

The clay figure whistled again. From all corners of the room, boxes began to rustle, drawers started to rattle and shelves began to shake. Out came an industrial-sized army of workers made from clay, ready to get to work.

"Wow! Look at this lot!" said Mary, pointing.

"Will this do?" asked Mr Tiggle-Trotter.

"Definitely," answered Frances.

"Then let's get to work."

And then he showed the clay people how to make all the things they were going to need.

Bundles of plain paper were ferried in along a line of clay workers and hoisted up onto the table. Assembly teams spread out and began to manufacture their parts. Once they had finished, the part was passed down to the next stage of the production line. Over and over again, paper would move along through the assembly process until the finished piece reached the inspection area. Each one was carefully inspected for any faults; not one was rejected.

Mr Tiggle-Trotter kept an eye on each process, saying, "Chariots next." Then he would change the instruction. "Horses now, we need more horses and more warriors." Over the top of their heads, he counted, "Three hundred and fifty-two – just the soldiers to make now."

"I say, we're doing splendidly well," declared Godfrey. "At this rate we're going to be done by midday."

"Ooh, just in time for another salad," said Mary, lost in her wishful thoughts.

The giant ape answered, in between counting. "Sorry – ten, twenty – we will – thirty, forty – be taking – fifty, sixty – a packed lunch – seventy, eighty – and supplies – ninety, a hundred – with us. It will take the rest of the day to get ready, and most of tomorrow to get to There."

"Where is 'there'?" asked Frances.

"No, Miss Frances, I think you are getting a bit mixed up," Godfrey said. "There is where we are going."

"But where is there, exactly?" asked Mary, clueless.

"I see what is happening here," smiled the giant ape. "There is a fertile region where the farmers grow their crops, called 'There'."

"Oh," gasped Frances. "There is where we are going. I get it now."

"What?" asked Mary, totally lost with the explanation.

Frances explained. "What is the village we live in called?"

"Head-Butt-No-Bacon," answered Mary, as it dawned on her. "There – oh yeah, so it is."

Mr Tiggle-Trotter's attention turned back to the book on origami. "Don't forget the weapons – we need more swords and spears, crossbows and arrows, please."

Standing on the tips of her toes, with her hand reaching for the sky, Mary stretched as much as she could. "I know," she squeaked, waving her arm. "What about water bombs?"

Flicking through the pages, the ape's giant fingers scanned the book. "There's nothing in here about water bombs."

"Miss Frances," began Godfrey, correcting his clothes, "do you know what water bombs are? More importantly, do you know how to make them?"

This was one of those times that Frances Fidget-Knickers was flummoxed, as she answered, "I have no idea – I've never seen one."

And this was one of those extremely rare moments in Mary's life that she knew something Frances didn't. With great pride, she started to show them how to make the bomb that you filled with water. Expertly, Mary Midget-Mouth folded the paper. "Look – it's quite easy really, once you know how. Just take a piece of square paper and fold it like this." Within seconds, the water bomb was made and Mary blew into it.

With great fascination, the giant ape studied the object. "It looks like a ball."

"That's exactly what it is," explained Mary, tapping on the hole she had just blown into. "This is where the water goes in."

The giant ape smiled. "Tactically, I think it will come in very useful, but we will need more than one."

"It's easy – really easy to do," Mary said, eagerly. "Frances and I could make them?" Like a shot, she turned to her friend and asked, "What do you think?"

Happily, Frances agreed, and the making of water bombs began. "Where did you learn to do this?" Frances asked.

"My uncle Herbert showed me," Mary answered. "He's my dad's brother – always telling me jokes and being silly. He's a real bundle of fun to be around."

Frances watched as her friend began to reveal the skill in folding sheets of paper. Soon, it looked like a deflated ball.

Frances' outstanding intellect instantly picked it up. Now presenting her first ever water bomb, she asked, "What do you think?"

"Blimey – you picked that up quick enough," gasped Mary. "It took me a few goes before I got the hang of it."

Godfrey smiled. "Well done, Miss Frances – and well done to you, Miss Mary, for being such a good teacher."

"Keep the ammunition coming – we will need a good supply to fend off the Snogg-Snifflers," said the giant ape. Running his finger through the line of moving paper, he stated, "Just over two thousand soldiers – plenty for what we will need."

The problem of transporting the origami army dawned on Frances. "How on earth are we going to get them all there?"

"Transportation will be provided," gestured the giant ape with his hand.

The clay figures were busy finishing the last of the paper wagons and horses. "How do you work that one out?" asked Mary. "They're just paper!"

"Miss Mary, all will become clear once we are on the move. But first, we will have to go poo-picking."

CHAPTER 13

PERMITS

Within minutes, the giant primate had picked everybody up. He moved swiftly down the corridor and out of the front door. Rushing across the white misty clouds, he hurried down the tree in a blur.

The forest floor rustled under Mr Tiggle-Trotter's feet as he began to walk. "Now, let's see, which way?" muttered the giant ape to himself.

Godfrey tapped the giant's hand with his cane. "I believe it is just down there," he said, using his walking stick to point the way.

"Where are we going?" asked Frances Fidget-Knickers.

Now supported by his cane, Godfrey stood to one side and answered, "To the post office; you can't go picking poo without the right documents in place."

"Why ever not?" asked Mary in an odd voice, the thought of scooping dung disagreeing with her.

"Because it belongs to someone else," answered the giant ape, "and that someone else is the Department for Magical Mixtures."

"Why would the Department for Magical Mixtures be interested in poo?" asked Frances.

"Because it has magical powers," answered Mr Tiggle-Trotter.

Godfrey wrinkled his nose, and those long whiskers twitched with the intake of air. "Let's not forget, it stinks to high heaven," insisted the rodent.

"That's the magic," answered the giant ape. "The more it stinks, the more powerful the spell."

"So let's get this straight," began Mary, feeling very uneasy about the task ahead. "We go to the post office … then we sign some documents … and then we go off to look for the smelliest poo we can find?" She stopped and screwed her nose up. "Has anyone thought this through properly? After all, it's supposed to be magic poo!"

Some branches snapped back as they moved through the forest. "Miss Mary, poo-handling can only be done safely and only with the right permits in place," Godfrey informed her. "Never try it without the correct paperwork."

Mary smirked. "I always make sure I use toilet paper – you don't want it getting under your fingernails, now, do you?"

Frances gasped with her eyes wide open, shocked but laughing at the same time. "Mary, that's gross!"

Mr Tiggle-Trotter spoke with a tone of uneasiness, ignoring the joke. "Very sorry state of affairs – nasty business, that Lord Snack-It, but kind of expected."

Frances became intrigued and asked, "What happened to him?"

"Miss Frances," said Godfrey, concern in his voice. "Magic has a way of knowing when things are not what they seem. Lord Snatch-It mistakenly thought his noble birth put him above the rest of us."

"Arrogance and misplaced pride got the better of him," agreed the giant ape.

"That it did," sighed Godfrey. "No permits, and the rest is history as they say."

"But what do they say?" queried Mary.

Mr Tiggle-Trotter answered. "That he vanished into thin air. Now he resides in the spirit world under lock and key for using magic without the right documents in place."

"Can you pass over to the spirit world?" Mary asked.

112

"Only if you are dead, Miss Mary," said Godfrey, with a shudder.

Mary mumbled to herself. "They want us to go poo-picking … magic poop at that … get a document … if the document's not correct … we will end up dead and imprisoned in the afterlife for all eternity." She looked up at the giant ape and said nervously, "Sounds fine to me – what could go wrong?"

"Good for you, Miss Mary," smiled Godfrey, not realising he was about to say something funny. "That's the spirit."

Frances and Mr Tiggle-Trotter laughed.

With a deadpan face, Mary grumbled, "Very funny, being dead would make me a spirit, I get it."

Godfrey chuckled. "Oh my, I made a joke and I didn't even know it."

While the rodent laughed, they moved on through the forest like some gigantic ice-breaker parting the trees. Then they approached a clearing. "Why aren't we going to Judge Get-It-Wrong to get our permits?" asked Frances Fidget-Knickers.

"Not enough time, as the court is a day's walk away," answered the giant ape, standing before a cave entrance so big that even he could enter.

In and out of the cave flew bats with customers' letters. Above the entrance was a sign that read: MR AND MRS STAMP-FILE-HER. They walked in.

Two very pale figures moved over the floor as if they were floating. Giving their instructions, one of them noticed they had customers. With dark eyes sunken deep into her sockets, and high cheek bones pulling in her skin, the lady spoke with what seemed like a Romanian accent.

"And what can I do for you?" she asked, exposing her canine teeth."

Mary made the play on words and stuttered, "Stamp-File-Hers … more like vampires?"

The lady moaned, and across came her husband. "My dear, take no notice – every now and then we have to expect that a rude customer will walk into our humble establishment."

Godfrey coughed and interrupted their moaning moment. "Mr and Mrs Stamp-File-Her, please forgive Miss Mary – she a visitor to these parts."

"Selena, my dear," spoke the gaunt-looking man. "An apology is given and we have work to do."

"Selena," said Frances. "That's a very pretty name. It's thought to come from the moon goddess. Although she was never a vampire, she was considered to be the mother of all modern vampires – not that I'm saying you are one."

"Ambrogio, my love," sighed his wife. "What are we to do? After all, she smells like a human."

"Ambrogio," chirped Frances. "That's the name of the famed vampire of legend, and means 'immortal' in Italian."

Mr Stamp-File-Her sniffed. "I smell two humans, my love. It looks like the game is up, my dear Selena. One day we knew this would happen, but I never thought it would be here, away from the world of humans."

Mr and Mrs Stamp-File-Her hugged each other, as if it was the last time they would ever see one another alive again.

"What are they doing?" asked Mary.

"I'm not sure," answered Frances, with a curious look. "Perhaps this is the way they greet customers in this world."

Godfrey became impatient and started to speak very briskly. "Excuse me, we are looking for the forms from the Department of Magical Mixtures. I wonder if you could point us in the right direction."

The strange-looking man gasped. "They are customers, after all! What am I thinking? Is this any way to greet a customer, my love?"

Mrs Stamp-File-Her slid out of the arms of her husband. "Forgive me – we thought you were someone else. It is not safe for us to be around humans. All they want to do is stick a wooden stake through our hearts."

"It's true," insisted Mr Stamp-File-Her. "We left that life many centuries ago and took up an honest day's work. We knew that one day if we stayed in the other world, Mr Stake-Driver would find us and plunge a wooden spike into our chests."

Then he changed into a bat and flew off.

"So I was right, then," shivered Mary, awkwardly. "You are vampires?"

"Of course we are, my dear child," replied the pale-looking woman, running her tongue over her teeth.

"Blinking hell," gulped Mary. "You're not going to bite me, are you?"

Mr Stamp-File-Her came flying back to his wife carrying the reddest of fruit, and changed back again. "Why would we want to do that when we have these lovely blood apples to eat?" he replied.

"You're fruit bats," gasped Frances, blinking in astonishment.

The princess of the night bit into the juicy apple and sucked it dry. "Thank you, my darling, it is most refreshing," she said happily. To Frances, she replied, "Of course we are, my young one. Now, my customers, what can I do for you?"

Mr Tiggle-Trotter knelt down, the hand everyone was in rested over his knee, and asked, "The form for spell-making – as given out by the Department for Magical Mixtures – could we have one, please?"

Mr Stamp-File-Her floated over to a rack of official-looking papers. "I have it right here. You are making mischief, I think?"

"Not as much as my grandfather," sighed Frances.

Taking the form from her husband, the fruit-sucking vampire asked, "Who is this person who makes such troubles for you? He is not using our post office. Speak now his name – we want to put him on our naughty list."

Spurting out the answer, Mary spluttered, "Granddad Sprinkle-Tinkle!"

The two servants of darkness clung to each in anguish, as Mr Stamp-File-Her cried, "My dearest Selena, I thought we would never hear of him again!"

His wife sighed sadly. "I know, my bravest of husbands – and after you were so brave, giving evidence at the trial."

Frances Fidget-Knickers realised her opportunity to ask a question. "I've hardly ever met anyone who was at my grandfather's trial. What do you know about him?"

With one awful shudder, the prince of darkness wept, "I curse the day we met him … and that Lord Snatch-It. I'm so glad Snatch-It has departed this world for the afterlife."

"My love, stop your tears," soothed his wife, caressing him. "If you want, I can tell the story?"

"My dearest Selena, you have always been my rock, but it is time I made a stand," he sobbed, going on with his tale to tell. "We were working away one day when Lord Snatch-It came into our humble place of work. With him was a baggy old bag of bones."

"That would be your grandfather," laughed Mary.

"Please – it is a painful enough story to tell. No interruptions if you please," sniffed Mr Stamp-File-Her. "Granddad Sprinkle-Tinkle was the man, and dark magic did he use on us." He stopped and trembled.

"You are doing splendidly, my love," smiled his wife, encouraging him to go on.

Drying his eyes, the vampire voice quivered. "Under the darkest of spells, we were forced to send forged documents to the Department for Magical Mixtures."

"My word," gasped Godfrey. "Forging official papers is a very serious offence."

"We know," gasped Mrs Stamp-File-Her. "To cover up those crimes, he must have had an accomplice to do his bidding."

"Did they catch him?" asked Frances.

"No," sighed Selena. "When all the arrests were made, that someone went to ground and was never found."

Swallowing hard from the nasty experience, her husband gulped. "It was horrible, my dear."

"The indignity of being clapped in irons," sighed Mrs Stamp-File-Her. "We pleaded our innocence, but no, they would not listen."

"My sweet Selena," sighed her prince, stroking her high cheekbones, "we have much to thank Mr Always-Wins-A-Case for. Sadly, he has retired now, and his son-in-law Mr Never-Won-A-Case has taken over from him."

117

"Yes, my dearest," shuddered his princess. "If it wasn't for him, we would have been imprisoned on Stinkers Island. And if it wasn't for Granddad Sprinkle-Tinkle, we would never have these awful memories."

Frances now put together some of the pieces to the puzzle. With the information in place, she spluttered, "That's it! He used the forged documents and someone at the Department for Magical Mixtures to help smuggle back enchanted potions. Why else can my parents not see his horrid ways?"

Waving the forms, Mr Stamp-File-Her insisted, "Together, we are making changes to his wicked ways."

"Do we have to?" sighed Mary. "Once those papers are signed, we're off poo-picking."

The nicest of female vampires smiled. "Not to worry – I can get you ladders, and sacks to put them in."

"Wait there – the sacks make sense to put the poo in," said Frances. "But the poo will be on the ground, so why do we need the ladders?"

The two post office workers exchanged odd glances as Godfrey spoke. "Miss Frances and Miss Mary, the poo is on the trees."

"Really?" gasped Mary, with an uneasy expression. "If it's not bad enough picking poo off the ground, we've got to go climbing trees as well for it!"

Mr Tiggle-Trotter decided it was time to enlighten them. "Poo is a fruit that hangs from branches."

Agreeing, Mr Stamp-File-Her smiled. "Is true – orchards are just a bat's wing away. What poo were you thinking of?"

Frances remembered a time when her awful grandfather did something very nasty. "Well," she began, "I was taking a shower in the bathroom, when my grandfather insisted on coming in, to do a number two."

"A number two?" puzzled Mr Stamp-File-Her. "What is this number two?"

Mary pointed to her backside and said, with a turned-up nose, "It comes out there and really smells."

Both vampires moaned with regret at asking the question. "It is stinky place," they protested.

"I'm glad we vampires don't breed," Selena said, "or I would be the one cleaning up after them."

Frances went on. "It was nasty and it really stank. It made me choke and cough, and all my grandfather said while I hid behind the shower curtain was ... 'that's a stinker, what a bowel-twitcher that was'."

The fang-wincing prince of the living dead gagged. "Please – enough of stinky talking. You must sign documents and put a stop to his dreadful behaviour."

Mrs Stamp-File-Her floated forwards and asked, "Which one of you is making your mark?" Then she changed into a bat, took hold of the papers to be signed and flew up to the giant ape's hand.

Searching his pocket as the flying vampire bat hovered, Godfrey pulled out a pen. "Let me," he said, scribbling his signature.

The bat returned to her husband and became a human figure once more. Then the two owners of the post office checked that all was well with the document.

"All is in order," smiled Mr Stamp-File-Her, stamping the paper. "Here are your permits, but first you must pay – you have coin?" Turning to his wife, he asked, "Selena, my fair one, would you mind handing these over and taking payment?"

Returning to the form of a bat, she landed on the giant's hand while changing back to herself again. Taking a gold coin from Godfrey, she bit into it and then examined the item. "No dents," she smiled, and she shouted to her husband, "We have been paid with good coin!" Then she returned to the ground and popped the payment into a cash register.

"That seems a bit strange. Why did she bite the money?" asked Mary Midget-Mouth.

With her immense amount of knowledge shining through, Frances answered. "In the olden days, they used to make fake money with lead and cover the coins in gold. If it was a fake coin, it would show an indent after you had bitten it."

Mr Tiggle-Trotter stood up and started to leave the post office. "Thank you for your time, Mr and Mrs Stamp-File-Her, and good day to you both."

"You are welcome," replied the vampires.

Mrs Stamp-File-Her waved them goodbye. "Please, you are good customers, so if there is anything you are wanting, then you are thinking of us, yes?" she smiled.

"You have good poo-picking time," they both said together, before turning into bats and going about their work.

CHAPTER 14

POO-PICKING

The giant ape picked up the pace, and the aroma of freshly picked poo was approaching before they knew it.

"Oh my," gasped Godfrey, his eyes watering. "I wish I had a failing sense of smell." With swift hands, he took out a tissue, tore it into pieces and stuffed them up each nostril. "That's better," he muttered, sounding like he had just caught a cold.

"I don't smell anything," said Mary.

Frances sniffed. "Me neither."

The giant primate smiled at the two girls and stated, "You humans have terrible senses."

Sounding like he was full of snot, Godfrey mumbled, "Any minute now – wait for it."

The orchard of trees bearing stinking fruit came into view, and over drifted a floating stench.

Frances caught it first and coughed. "That smells just like my grandfather after a number two."

Mary gagged and spluttered, "That's worse than my dad's stinky feet and pop-offs put together."

Mr TiggleTrotter put them down next to a hut.

As soon as they touched the ground, the door opened and out came the groundskeeper. "Now then," he muttered to himself, holding a clipboard and taking a pen from behind his ear. "Must make sure to plant more seedlings and clear those leaves over at …" He stopped as he caught sight of them. "Well, then, I don't know how I missed you lot, especially the size of the big fellow there," he jested. "Here for a bit of sightseeing? Or could it be happy hour?"

"Neither," answered Godfrey. "We're here for a spot of poo-picking."

"Well, then," chirped the groundskeeper cheerfully, "you'll be needing some sacks." Looking up at the giant ape, he apologised. "Sorry, big fella, you will have to wait here. We can't have you trampling on the trees." Turning back to Godfrey, he asked, "Have you got the permits?"

"Right here," said the rodent, handing them over.

"I see Mr and Mrs Stamp-File-Her have stamped it," the man wheezed, making sure all was in order. "At night I sometimes watch them fly by the light of the moon. Lovely couple, but talk a bit funny, don't you think?"

"That's because they're vampires," said Mary.

"Vampires, you say?" sniffed the groundskeeper, without a care in the world. "Haven't got the slightest inkling as to what a vampire is. Sound foreign to me … that would explain it." The permits were given back, along with some sacks as he pointed nearby. "You'll see there are some ladders to use already down there. Well, got to get on – try not to drop any crushed ones … or I'll have problems with the leaves."

The giant primate sat himself down while the other three walked off.

Walking down the dirt track, Frances giggled. "I really thought we were going to be picking animal dung."

"I still don't like the idea of the smell," sniffed Mary. "It's getting worse."

The offensive pong really hit them hard as they entered the orchard. Its foul odour made their eyes water. "Here you go, Miss Frances and Miss Mary," winked Godfrey, handing over some leftover tissue. "Stick this up your noses; it might help with the unpleasant fragrance."

122

Now with all three of their noses stuffed full of tissue, they made a start at picking the poo while sounding like they had all caught the flu.

"Oh my," coughed Godfrey, running up a ladder. "It certainly has a perfumed atmosphere all of its own." Climbing off the piece of equipment, he scrambled over the branches and picked its fruit. "Miss Frances and Miss Mary, I think it might be best you stay out of the way. Just pick up the ones I throw down."

A few poo fruits were tossed to the ground, and the two girls ran around doing as they were asked. The distinctive pong was especially unpleasant, as Mary gagged, "I don't know if this tissue is doing much good stuck up my nose."

"It really stinks," choked Frances, stuffing the poo into a sack.

Suddenly, a pelting of fruit came down as Godfrey shook the branches. "Look out below!" he shouted.

The poo rained down on them and some of the poo fruit split open, releasing its foulness. Frances and Mary had extreme difficulty in breathing as the stench constricted their airways.

"Miss Frances and Miss Mary," shouted Godfrey, as the branches stopped shaking, "I would avoid the ones that have split open. I don't think you would tolerate the smell."

With their restricted passageways blocking fresh air from reaching their lungs, they gagged even more for air.

Frances managed a loud cry. "Thanks for the information, but I kind of figured that one out!"

Godfrey gave the tree limbs another shake. "I think that will be enough," he panted as the branches rustled, releasing more poo to the ground. "Just give me a few seconds and I will be straight back down. Oh, I nearly forgot – the magic is in the juice of the fruit."

Mary choked as she saw something move under the sacks. "Look at that!" she cried.

The repugnant poo juice oozed out of the over-ripened fruit and onto the leaves. Now the magic began, making things that shouldn't move move. Up stood the leaves, stretching, and walked around as though they were living creatures.

Frances and Mary just stared at their feet as the leaves approached them.

"What do we do?" asked Mary anxiously.

"I don't know," answered Frances awkwardly.

Godfrey stepped from the last rung of the ladder and said to the two girls, "I thought that might happen." Now with his attention on the leaves, he asked, "Would you mind picking up the fruit, and popping them in the sack for us?"

And that's exactly what the leaves did.

"So that's how it works," sighed Frances, with a relaxing release of breath. "We're going to use the poo juice to make the origami army come alive."

"Correct, Miss Frances," answered Godfrey, watching the leaves rolling the poo into piles.

Releasing her anxiety, Mary cried in surprise, "That's fantastic!"

"It is, isn't it, Miss Mary?" agreed Godfrey, as the sacks were filled. "I think we've got enough now. Shall we make our way back to Mr Tiggle-Trotter?"

Each of them had a sack of poo over their shoulders and they headed back up the dirt track. "What about the leaves?" asked Frances, wheezing as she spoke.

"The magic only lasts for a day," answered Godfrey, treading over the uneven ground. "As soon as night falls, the leaves will become normal leaves again."

As the leaves took a well-earned rest, Mary, with a rattling sound in her chest, wheezed with gratitude, "Thanks for the help."

Adjusting his sack, Godfrey smiled. "Just as well we have extra supplies; you never know what might happen in the heat of battle."

Now they approached the giant ape and they were taken by his huge hand. Swiftly they started to make their way back to his house. "We need to get to the farms before the Snogg-Snifflers do," he stressed, racing through the forest. "We will be leaving bright and early tomorrow morning, so it's going to be an early night for all of us."

CHAPTER 15

MARCHING

While Frances and the others were all in bed, the Snogg-Sniffler army was on the march. They had set off by the light of a full moon.

That was twelve hours ago now, and the lush green farms were coming into view.

"We is almost there," shouted the Sniffler in charge of the royal coach. Taking the whip from behind his shoulder, he cried out and let the line crack forwards. "You is not going fast enough, you is quickening now!"

With a snapping sound, the leather struck a Snogg-Sniffler across its back. "Ouch!" he winced. Then he turned to look at the driver. "I is having you for ill-treatment," he snorted.

Another lash came striking down on the complaining porker, as the sound of the cracking faded. "You is just the same as rats! If you is not doing good job then you is all going in the pot as well! Me, personally, I is liking you all roasted and crispy, as all the fat is making lovely pork drippings … scrumptious!" smiled the driver.

The shamed commander at the very front struggled to pull the royal carriage. Talking to his troops, he spluttered, "You does stained my reputation. You does all pull harder. I does not want any more blemishes on my career."

Walking next to the commander, the second in command agreed. "You lot is doing a disservice to our King, and now you is lazy pulling."

A few of the disgraced beasts started to whisper.

"I is having a think," grumbled one of them.

"What is your thinking?" they asked in low voices.

"My brain thought is telling me that we is all being chopped and diced, ready for the pot, if we is not faster pulling."

"We is not wanting that," went the whispering.

"What is we doing about it?" asked one of them.

The thinking Snogg-Sniffler said, "Impressing our King, we is. So we is upping our pace to fast trotting, and from fast trotting to full galloping."

With a transfer of glances they all agreed, and then gave their blessing to the Snogg-Sniffler who had come up with the brainy thought. "You is saying when," they grinned.

"I be doing that," he grunted.

With secret winks and nods, the hogs made ready for a change in speed.

Meanwhile, with no inkling of what was about to happen, the commander chatted to the second in command. "Me is summarising, and I has come to conclusion we is needing to put troops through more training exercises."

Before the lower-ranked officer could answer, a very loud instruction was bellowed out: "When!"

With the green light now given, slowly the momentum picked up pace. "What is you doing?" scrambled the commander, almost falling over.

"We is exercise training," came a reply, "and you is included."

"That's more like it!" yelled the Sniffler in charge of the hog-drawn carriage. With a crack of the whip, he cried, "You does have more in the tank than that! You is only halfhearted trying! You is picking your hooves up now!"

With a snort and a glance, a voice hollered back, "We is showing you how fast-stepping we can be!" The hollering head of the hog turned back to encourage the others. "Come on, we is doing better than this!"

All the beasts got the bit between their teeth and skyrocketed to almost full speed.

The coach driver was taken completely by surprise. The sudden outburst of acceleration whisked him up like a kite. With his body now in mid-air, and hanging on to the reins, he shouted, "Whoopee, we is moving now! Me is thinking the King is happy with whooshing speed!"

Inside the carriage, his royal highness bumped about like a bag of mad frogs. "You has to admit," he declared, in between bouncing, "this be a smooth ride."

Granddad Sprinkle-Tinkle hung on to anything that would stop him from rebounding around inside the coach. "Jeepers!" he cried. "Golly!" he gasped.

"I is seeing you is impressed with speediness," smiled the King. "My Snifflers are putting a bit of oomph power into it."

"Shucks," replied the bundle of old bones, "I never would have guessed."

"That's what I is thinking, so I is letting you know about breakneck speed. You is holding on better, we is going for top gear now," informed the King as he shouted out, "Faster – I is wanting quick-as-a-wink speeding!"

Outside, the obedient coach driver took a few moments before he shouted.

These few moments gave the commander enough time to gasp, "I is needing more fitness working!"

"Not to worry," said the second in command, catching his breath. "If you is not keeping up, they is backside-kicking you. And you is falling down, and they is trampling over you, then you is under wheels of carriage, bumpy bump, you is going, wheels is cutting you in half, and we is leaving you behind in two pieces."

The commander gave a quick look at his junior officer. "I is lucky my wife is good at sewing, but I is not liking prickly needles, so I is harder trying."

At that moment, the driver screamed out, "Winking-quick speeding the King wants!"

"Whoosh" went the coach as it reached full speed.

Back inside the carriage, the King hit his head very hard against the wooden roof. It didn't hurt. "Now where was I?" he smiled. "I is liking bumping-fast speed, what is you thinking?"

Granddad Sprinkle-Tinkle was beginning to lose his grip as he panicked. "Hold on! Keep hold of it!" he stressed, followed by a grumbling moan. "Why me? Me bones are rattling faster than a rattlesnake." Before he lost his grip, he concluded, "And they make a right racket." Then the villainous old man went boomeranging around the carriage. First he hit the floor with a thud. "AGHHH!" he cried out, only to be jettisoned up to the ceiling with an enormous bumping bounce. "Crack" went his bones. "AGHHH!" he screamed, as his shoulder was dislocated while falling on the King.

"Sound like you has broken something," frowned the King of the Snogg-Snifflers. "I is trained in first-aiding – let me help you up." Then he gave a good, stiff whack to the old grump's back.

"Click" went Granddad Sprinkle-Tinkle's shoulder as it went back into place. "AGHHH, OUCH, OUCH, AGHHH!" he cried, with real tears of pain.

"See, what is I telling you? You is sounding good as new with clicking noise," spoke the royal Snogg-Sniffler, checking for more bodily injuries. "You is all baggy. And you is all saggy. We is needing to harden you up, so you is travel-bumping okay. I is holding you now, so you is not getting hurt."

The carriage heaved from side to side. As the wheels hit a lump in the ground, it lurched forwards, sending the King, who was holding Granddad Sprinkle-Tinkle, hurtling to the floor.

The belly flop was nasty.

The King was very heavy.

And the repellant old man got squashed.

"Me guts!" he cried out in agony.

"You is excusing me," apologised the monarch, "but that is move we first-aiders do when you is all blocked up and not pooping properly."

Another ridge was hit and the pair of them were tossed up and came back down, with the King landing on the horrid old man's chest. "AGHHH, GURGLE, COUGH, SPLUTTER!" he winced out through gritted teeth.

"Again, you is excusing me," apologised the monarch, looking down. "That is first-aiding move for when Snifflers are doing doggy paddle wrong."

A patch of smooth ground gave them time to get to their feet, as another sudden bump sent the King and the old man crashing forwards.

This time, Granddad Sprinkle-Tinkle ended up on top of the King of the Snogg-Snifflers. "You is not my wife," the regal one grumbled. "I am not having tomfoolery in my carriage with a stranger. After all, you is all skinny and yucky-looking."

All the old man could do was yelp as he was thrown off. "Help!" he cried.

Outside, there came cries from the beasts pulling the royal coach.

"Look, see – we is nearing now!"

"I is seeing nothing, but my snout is telling me we is getting closer!"

"Is you thinking our King is being pleased with us making good, quick timing?"

The driver, his body still dangling in the wind like a kite, cried out, "You is slowing now!"

With great relief, the commander puffed, "I is glad we is reducing speediness, as I was almost on my last legs."

A dimwit of a hog stated, "I is only having one set of legs."

Speaking with his thoughts, a twit of a boar answered back, "I is thinking when you is officer material, you is getting more than two legs."

The dimwit replied, "Then I is training up to be an officer, as these ones are nearly ready for the bin."

Back inside the carriage, Granddad Sprinkle-Tinkle made half-hearted groans. "Haaa, eek, squeak," went the sounds.

131

His royal highness noticed the change in speed, but made no sense of the moaning noises. "You is stopping with your gaga talking – we is coming to a stop," he grunted.

The coach driver scrambled down and opened the door. "We is here, Our Illustrious One," he said with a bow. "Has you recuperated nicely from rickety, dumpty journey?"

"I is under-prepared," declared the King, rubbing the royal middle. "I is wanting a dumping."

With a quick mind-jogging tut, the coach driver informed his highborn passenger, "Remember what your wife is saying when you is out with the other Snifflers? No bringing home all that crass and nasty talking ways, Your Majesty."

"You is right," sighed the King, changing his words. "I has a package ready." Then he gave his orders to two beasts. "You is both digging hole for the royal do-doings."

The hole was dug and the King walked over to it. "You is all turning your backs," he insisted. "You is not sneaky-peaking at my problem area."

They all turned.

They all listened.

And they all heard some horrible windy bottom noises as the King strained.

"Out you is going," he muttered.

"In you is not staying," he stuttered.

Gasping, he carried on with the bottom work.

"I is making big job," he grunted.

"Me is almost done," he strained.

When he had finished, he announced proudly, "I has sent my parcel!"

Then he walked away, leaving a very big poo behind.

After the roaring died down, Granddad Sprinkle-Tinkle stepped out of the carriage, with the appearance of someone who'd been dragged through a hedge backwards. Some of the tumbling had crushed a couple of folds of mucous membrane stretching across the inside of his throat. Twanging unlike before, a faint, husky whisper sounded from his voice box. "Outrageous – simply an unacceptable way to travel," he moaned.

The King walked towards his army and roared, "We is stopping here to be rested! After a good feeding and sleeping, then, when we is waking up in the morning, we is breakfasting and fighting ... what is you all saying to that?"

Granddad Sprinkle-Tinkle took cover under the royal coach as the rush and crush of a fiesta of fun started.

With a clashing of heads, one of them cried out, "You is watching those tusks, or you does poke my eye out!"

"Stop with your chum-chummy ways and get down to partying!" cried the reply.

"I is hopping and bopping like never before!" yelled a porker, spinning around and hitting anyone in reach.

"You does need to chillax," groaned one of the hogs who had just been whacked.

"I is agreeing," huffed a very large Snogg-Sniffler. Then he sent out a pulverising blow, sending the hopping and bopping boar over the heads of all of them.

As he whistled through the air, the punch-drunken hog looked down and mumbled, "I is taking some time out now," and hit the ground with a thud.

Bending down, the King smiled at the trembling bag of old bones. "A bit of brinkmanship," he grinned, with great joy. "I is liking it when we is pushing it to the limit."

"You do? I mean, of course you do," agreed Granddad Sprinkle-Tinkle.

"It be emotionally draining being the King – always discreet with my message-making and what nots," he sighed. "I know – I is having a bit of merry-making! It does not be correct diplomatic way for a king to behave, but it does be cheering me up." Happily, he bundled in, and the royal fists went smashing into anything. Rib-punches, back-scratching, leg-kicks and elbow-smashing of face were just some of the things the King did. "I is having a hooting good time," bellowed his most happy of royal highnesses.

Clinging to one of the coach wheels, Granddad Sprinkle-Tinkle peered at the celebrating Snogg-Snifflers through the spindles, his face changing colour in disbelief. "This is going to take some getting used to, but it's better than going back to that other world," he muttered to himself.

Along with the merry-making, the Snifflers started to sing a horrid song.

"Baa, baa, black sheep, I is making it red wool," went a rejoicing boar as the tune carried on.

"Tomorrow we is having moo-moo hooves and all," frolicked another hog in his deep voice.

Finishing the ditty, a beast sang, "Not forgetting giddy-ups made into stew."

The king staggered back to Granddad Sprinkle-Tinkle. "We is having fantastic jolly-ups," he slobbered, pulling out a couple of teeth. "Driver – where be my metal replacements?"

A large bag of metal assortments was handed over. Rummaging around inside, the King took out two gold structures, and the incisor and canine teeth were hammered into the jaw bone. "How is I looking?" he asked, grinning at the old man.

A sparkle of greed, with a sprinkling of sucking-up took over, as Granddad Sprinkle-Tinkle hissed sneakily, "I like your gum-knives – with choppers like that, a pittance of a dinner will never be yours."

"I has tried all sorts, but these is not sending my mouth manky," sniffed the King, sucking his lips over them. "They is nice and shiny, and I is not having peasants' meal with my gum-munching."

"That's because they're gold," the old man slyly answered, with the chance of empire-building coming to his mind. "Do you have much of it?"

The reigning monarch tossed the bag over to the most devious of grandfathers. "We is having tons of the stuff," shrugged the King, carelessly. "Not much good for weapons-making. But they does make good mouth cones."

135

Greedily rubbing his hands, the crooked old man said, "But, Your Majesty, with this you can buy more farms than there are farms to buy."

With a dignified grunt, the King of the Snogg-Snifflers commented, "Where be the fun in that? We is hogs, and Snifflers is liking slam, bang, walloping ways."

Eagerly, the old man spluttered, "Your Majesty, I have tons of gold as well, and I stashed mine in some caves in the red desert. So if we are putting it together, we could buy the whole of this world."

"I is supposing you might be onto something," grunted the King, "but we is still want our battling tomorrow."

"Tomorrow, the farms – after that, the world," hissed the horrid old man.

The King yawned. "We is resting up now. I is always persecuting better on a good night's sleep."

CHAPTER 16

CLAY OFFICERS

The journey had been a long and dusty one. Preparations were now under way to make ready for the next day. The lifeless origami army had been unloaded and stacked in neat rows away from the fires.

Aside from the cooking pots, two bubbling cauldrons spluttered out their stench.

Nearby, a sack of poo was opened.

In the cauldron the fruit went.

The water hissed and spat.

"That really stinks – won't the Snogg-Snifflers smell this?" coughed Mary.

Gradually, the hissing and spitting died down as the simmering sound of cooking took over. The easterly wind gently carried the scent in the direction of the distant camp fires, where the beasts were plotting carnage of grotesque proportions.

"If their snouts are as sensitive as you say," stared Frances, looking over the grassland, "I would think they already can."

"Miss Frances and Miss Mary, seeing as we've worked so hard, it wouldn't hurt if we skipped cleaning up before supper," said Godfrey.

The two girls put down whatever they were doing and raced over to one of the cooking pots. "Let's get some grub!" cried Mary.

A clay officer scratched its head, as Frances and Mary held out their bowls.

Godfrey went over to a different cooking pot; his bowl was filled, and then he sat down. "Vegetable soup," he sniffed. Then he slurped a spoonful. "It's soooo refreshing, my compliments to the chef," he smiled, with a satisfying slurp.

Now the two girls prompted the puzzled-looking clay officer.

Their bowls were filled

"It looks disgusting," said Mary, as the dollop went in.

"Don't forget that's what you thought about the anything-you-like salad," Frances reminded her friend. "Mind you, it doesn't look very nice."

The meal in front of them resembled a mix of oats and wallpaper paste. Looking more like porridge, it smelt of watered-down disinfectant.

Mary went first and, with only a fraction of a second's separation, Frances followed, as they took their first spoonfuls together.

In an instant, the brain receptors sent out their messages.

And faster than it went in, the food was spat out in disgust.

"That's awful!" gagged Frances.

"It's revolting!" spat Mary.

A tapping noise was made by the clay officer who had dished up their meal. He started to move his hands and fingers.

"I say," said Godfrey, recognising the hand movements. "The dear chap is using sign language."

While talking in sign, the clay officer shifted around the pot annoyingly.

"What's he saying?" asked Mary.

"I don't know," answered Frances.

"Oh my, that is funny," chuckled Godfrey, as he signed back at the officer. "You don't say. It's hardly surprising."

"What's surprising?" inquired Frances.

"How's it funny?" asked Mary.

Godfrey giggled.

The giggle turned into laughter.

Then the laughter turned back to a giggle.

Still talking in sign language, the rodent chuckled. "Apparently, you're eating the medical supplies. Those supplies are going to be used tomorrow to patch up the paper soldiers if they get injured." Godfrey then made a scooping movement towards his mouth and some heaving movements with his body, and pretended to throw up.

The clay officer buckled over with laughter.

"Hurrah, very funny," said Mary sarcastically.

"Oh, look – he's asking if you want some more," giggled Godfrey.

"Whoopee do," said Mary, again with a hint of sarcasm.

Two clay figures walked over and exchanged the bowls of medical paste for vegetable soup. With enthusiasm and thanks, they were gratefully received.

"This smells better," said Frances.

"That's more like it," sniffed Mary.

"Tuck in!" cried Godfrey.

The anticipation of something extraordinary happening with the meal came to an abrupt end. "It's just vegetable soup," Mary said, rather disappointed. "Just like my mum's, actually."

"Your mum's soup is lovely," insisted Frances, recalling a time she had lunch at her friend's house. "It's better than my grandfather's, any day."

"Miss Frances and Miss Mary, these are army rations," said Godfrey. "We can't expect luxuries on the eve of hostilities."

Suddenly, there came an almighty splattering from the cauldron as the clay officers tipped in more poo fruits.

Instantly, everyone turned.

Everyone watched.

Everyone held their noses.

Then they all covered their mouths.

The harvested poo bubbling away really stank.

"Blimey, that stinks," coughed Frances, "and I thought it couldn't get any worse than when we first picked them."

"You got that wrong," gagged Mary.

As the clay officers stood ready with their flasks, Godfrey, his nostrils held tight with forefinger and thumb, got up to help with the enchanted brew. "There you go," he winced.

Once the canteens were filled, the clay people made towards the army made from paper. Instructions were given by pointing. "Here, here and here, if you please," ordered the giant ape.

As usual, Mary's thoughts came blurting out. "This won't work! It can't work! You said that when nightfall comes, they all go back to being just leaves – and won't this happen with the paper army?"

"Miss Mary, you're quite right, I did say that," acknowledged Godfrey. "But I have added a little something extra to sweeten the pot. Like some other fruits, the dietary fibre is found in the skins, so I've left them on."

"I see," Frances said, "Like grapes and apples?"

Godfrey shuddered. "Well, Miss Frances, you wouldn't want to eat these skins – they'll give you bad breath. These peels are rich in essential oils. The oil glands are spread all over the skins, giving off the fruit's obnoxious aroma, which gives the mixture the extra kick we need."

The clay officers kept returning for more of the magical mixture.

"There, there and over there," instructed the giant ape, as the army came to life.

Frances, Mary, and not forgetting Godfrey, all watched.

Mr Tiggle-Trotter gave more orders. "Here for chariots. There for horses. Come along – army personnel and carts towards me, if you please."

During the moments between orders and watching, columns of soldiers stood waiting. They waited until all of them were ready. Now at full strength, the army of folded paper figures stood to attention as the giant ape asked, "Frances, would you mind shaking the box and asking for some shovels?"

"I can do that," she replied, giving the box a rattle. "Could we please have some spades?"

The box spat out a deck of playing cards. "I think it might be broken," gasped Mary, spreading out the cards. "They're all the same suit – spades, would you believe it?"

"Try again, Miss Frances," urged Godfrey, "but this time, be more specific."

"Okay, I'll give it a go – but how many do we need?" she asked.

The answer shocked her.

"Two thousand and three, plus two thousand and three baskets," answered the great ape.

Frances gasped and raised her eyebrows.

Making sure to get her words right, Frances Fidget-Knickers asked, "Could we please have some shovels and baskets, and could you make the quantity two thousand and three of each, please?"

"Quick march," ordered Mr Tiggle-Trotter, as the box started to churn out the order.

In orderly rows, the paper soldiers maintained their proper distance and took a shovel and basket each as they passed the box. Maintaining their discipline, they were organised back into uniformed rows by the clay officers. With rhythmic steps, they kept their code and quick-marched away.

Looking on as the horses pulled the carts, Mary whispered, "I didn't like to say anything, but shouldn't they be taking weapons?"

Frances Fidget-Knickers went to answer, but before she could do so, the giant ape stated, "Preparation – our basic mobility tomorrow will depend on it."

Mary shook her head. "What does that all mean?"

"It's top secret, Miss Mary," answered Godfrey, as another column of soldiers took up their shovels. "Idle chit-chat costs lives."

142

"Excuse me?" asked Mary.

Frances spoke very quietly. "I think he means we might have some spies in our midst."

"Oh," reacted Mary nervously, unable to manage more than a one-word answer.

As the last of the soldiers took up their equipment, Godfrey muttered softly, "They're off on a secret mission."

"What are they going to do?" asked Mary, saying the words softly under her breath.

Frances shrugged her shoulders. "I don't know – it's a secret," she replied.

The giant ape was now whispering his secret orders to the clay officers. Every now and then he would pause, and then start to whisper again. His thoughts deep into military manoeuvring, he took very little notice of anyone.

After quite some time, silence fell over the camp as the giant primate walked over and sat down. He talked of many things, but the battle the next day was not discussed. The sound of digging could be heard as the origami army prepared for war.

"We should all get some rest now," yawed Mr Tiggle-Trotter. "We're going to need all our strength in the morning."

CHAPTER 17

THE BATTLE BEGINS

"Wake ups, I is telling you," kicked a Snogg-Sniffler. "I is
the knocker-upper."

"You is leaving me be," grumbled the booted hog. "I is
having wonderful dreams."

"I is reliable," stated the knocker-upper. "I is best
waking-upper there is."

"I is not caring," moaned the tired beast. "I is back with
my dreaming."

"I is knocking you ups," the first Snogg-Sniffler replied,
as he put the boot in. "You is rousing from your sleepy
time. No more is you slumbering – we has a war to attend."

In the blink of an eye, the rib-kicked Snogg-Sniffler stood to his feet. "We is," he stretched. "Why does you not say in the first place? I does help you with the rousing-time."

The mere mention of combat, after the knocker-upper and his newly found helper had hit all of the sleeping beasts, was enough to bring them to their hooves. Together, the army of Snogg-Snifflers crept over to where their king and Granddad Sprinkle-Tinkle were sleeping.

"You is all helping me with alarm-calling," whispered the knocker-upper. "We is all knowing it be safer in numbers, as our King is moody in the mornings. On the count of three, we is saying the waking words."

The count was started.

"One," they all whispered, looking uneasy.

"Two," they all mumbled, trying not to look nervous.

"Three," they all hushed, after which they yelled out, "Wakey-wakey, Your Majesty!"

Granddad Sprinkle-Tinkle jumped out of his skin. "HAAA!" he cried out in a sudden state of awakened panic.

The King turned over and opened one eye. "I is only half woken," he yawned, rubbing his hand over his left ear.

145

"Right you is, Our Magnificent One," winked the knocker-upper, turning to the army. "We is only doing half a job. So we is shouting some more, and we is making it thunder-shouting loud."

This time, they all yelled out at the very tops of their voices. "WAKEY-WAKEY, YOUR MAJESTY!"

Granddad Sprinkle-Tinkle cupped his ears to fend off the bellowing sound. "I hate mornings," he moaned.

The King opened the other eye and sniffed. "I is fully woken ups, now."

An ill-mannered hog stepped forwards. "Is you wanting your whipping Sniffler so you can beats him?" he asked, leaning in towards his majesty. "You is unreasoning in the mornings until you has punch someone."

"I is not," answered the King, sending out a crunching blow. "You is doing just fine."

The beast dropped like a stone from the blow.

Stepping over the body, the shamed commander groveled. "Your Anointed One, I is asking if me and my Snifflers is saving face. I has fifty of the fastest troops in the whole army."

At that moment, the King was being helped to his feet. "Not the nifty-fifty?" he gasped. "They is shifty-quick company of Snifflers. What is you proposing?"

The commander began with his strategy. "We is being naughtier than naughty."

"You is?" inquired the King.

"We is making big mischievous happenings," stated the commander.

"You does?" asked the King.

Smiling, the armed leader declared, "I is saying there isn't anything my troops won't be wrecking."

The monarch smiled.

With a rolling of his hand, he indicated the welcome to come closer.

"I is liking the plan so far – you is quick-stepping this way."

The armed leader stepped forwards.

Now in between his monarch and the horrid old man, the commander insisted, "We is not taking any churchy-do-gooders. If they is boo-hooing with blubbering tears, we is head-whacking them … that does shut them up."

"This plan be getting better. I is liking it more and more," beamed the King, with a royal grunt.

Granddad Sprinkle-Tinkle grinned nastily. "Me too," he hissed.

With an instructing movement to show the King how he would be signalling that all was ok, the commander waved his arm. "Then we does give signal like this, so you does know it be safe to come forwards. And then you is all having fast, takeaway farm food. But we is needing Him. Him is only one who does have good seeing eyes," he stated.

Taken completely by surprise, Granddad Sprinkle-Tinkle spluttered, "I'm not built for speed…"

A roar of approval boomed out. "Splendid plan! You has the job! And Him is going with you!"

The old man was quickly taken by the nifty-fifty. Comforting cries and heartening cheers embraced them all as they marched out of camp.

"We is eliminating look-outs!" they cried.

"Then we is hammering home our advantage!" they sang.

The commander leading the niftiest of the Snogg-Snifflers welcomed the high spirits. "I is inspired," he proudly announced, grabbing the old man. "We is camouflaging like colour-changing lizards and then we is pummelling."

"How does it happen?" whined Granddad Sprinkle-Tinkle. "How? How, I'm asking?"

With uneven breathing, the second in command stated, "You is boot-licker. All back-scratchers is getting first choices. I is a yes-Sniffler, with my back-slapping and flattering, but I does get nowhere."

"What can I say?" wriggled the old man, as they crawled through the undergrowth. "You're either born lucky or you're not. At this moment, I wish I was going in the opposite direction."

"You is a natural," said a beast. "You is good at brown-nosing."

Another hog chipped in. "Perhaps if I is doormat or hanger-on, I is up for promotion to lackey. Maybe I is razzle-dazzle a bit more, what does you reckon?"

"You buffoon," grunted the commander. "You is buttoning lips." Then he sniffed. "I is smelling enemy. Him, up you is getting, and looking is what you is doing."

Granddad Sprinkle-Tinkle peered over the grass. "It's a nightmare," the old man quivered, as he tried to count. "There are hundreds, maybe thousands," he squirmed.

"Quick – you is pulling Him down," whispered the second in command.

With a quick tug, he was pulled to the floor.

On the way down, he fainted.

"Humans," sniffed the commander, in contempt. "Who is having best eyes for seeing now?"

"He is," pointed several fingers.

"I is checking first," snorted the second in command, holding up his hand. "How many fingers is I showing?"

Eyes straining with the effort, the chosen Sniffler answered, "Only as many as you is wanting me to see."

"Excellent," smiled the commander. "You is our chief look-out. You is up ahead scouting. You does let us know what you is seeing, and you does send back the information with your secret shouting messages. Off you is going now."

The chief spotter got up and ran forwards. "I is not seeing much yet!" he yelled.

"That's good intel," stated the second in command, as another shout came back.

"I is still checking!" shouted the scout, as he woke the old man up with his ear-piercing cry.

"That is being remarkable intelligence work," smiled the commander. "And it does be clear and loud receiving."

The old man listened.

"All clear – you is coming now!" beckoned the scout, with a yodelling cry.

All of them edged forwards.

Granddad Sprinkle-Tinkle, with his cowardly ways, tried to stay put. "Just in case they try to surround us, I will stay here."

A lolloping Snogg-Sniffler came through and scooped up the old bag of bones. "We is under royal orders so you does not get hurt. We has no nerve to disobey our King, so you is coming with us."

Up in front, the scout shouted, "My eyes is wearing out with gazing! I is needing replacements before they does fall out!"

Making a hollow sound, the commander gurgled to Granddad Sprinkle-Tinkle, "Him, you is showing extra courage. You is getting peerage if you is succeeding. We is staying here now."

The lower-ranking officer chipped in, "We is making sure you has good fighting chance so we is sending with you Pick-It, Roll-It and Flick-It. They is the best of the best, and we is happier if they is with you."

Secret shouts were sent out, and the It brothers came over. "You is protecting Him. Now off you is going," instructed the commander.

The brothers decided to have a little family chat before they carried out their orders. "I is not having a penny bean," wiggled Pick-It, picking his nose. "I is all dried up."

"If that be so," whimpered Roll-It with empty hands, "then I is not making snotty ammunition."

"Without my boggy bullets, we is useless," sniffed Flick-It, having a sudden idea. "I is knowing – we is always using pointy weapons. Is we all up for a bit of skullduggery?"

They all smiled, and then Pick-It answered. "I is having fire-bubbling blood surging through my veins, I is taking spears."

"My blood pressure is almost at bursting point," wheezed Roll-it through clenched teeth. "I is more for tradition – I is taking truncheon, as I does like a bit of bludgeoning."

Flick-It snorted. "I is liking to send a chill-axe down their backs. With any luck, they be frozen stiff in fear and I be splitting them in two … we is off now!"

The weapons were taken and Granddad Sprinkle-Tinkle asked, "Don't I get one to protect myself with?"

A teeny-weeny dagger was handed over. "Here you is," laughed Pick-It. "You is being careful, now, as you has not much experience in battling."

"Don't cuts yourself," teased Roll-It, "or they is following your blood trail and catching you."

Flick-It looked at the old man with a worried face. "We does be responsible for your safety. If we does any mismanaging … we is being spiked on poles."

Their commanding officer huffed, "Enough talking with your impaling speak. You is getting on with it now."

"Okay!" they all answered.

With a squeeze, they took hold of Granddad Sprinkle-Tinkle and shot forwards. "You're hurting me arm," complained the old man.

"We is hurting more than that if we is displeasing the King," they all agreed, tugging at the ancient bundle of body parts.

The nasty old man moaned on. "Don't you go forgetting I'm the one with the brains!"

They heard the scout shuffling as they broke through the last remaining strands of high grass. "You has made it," he breathed, sniffing the air. "We has many enemies in front – I is detecting large swellings in their ranks."

All four hogs stood, their snouts sniffing in the breeze.

"Him, what is you seeing?" asked the chief scout.

The origami army had been busy all night long and the obstacles now in place were many. Fortifications made from enormous quantities of earth dug out of the ground rose up to become formidable defences. The pits left behind were hidden from site, ready to trap anyone that dared cross over their path.

"I can see barricades," answered the trembling old wreck.

"What is they looking like?" asked Pick-It, finger-wiggling his nostril and sighing, "Nope … still dry."

"It's a fortress made from mud," the old man gasped in shock.

"How big is it being?" asked Roll-It, inspecting his dry hands. "I is needing some mucus-moisturising," he sighed.

"About the same size as the King's castle," answered Granddad Sprinkle-Tinkle over the moans of Roll-It.

"That be almost impregnable," gulped Flick-It, practising his finger-flicking without much success. "I is losing my touch," he sniffed.

Now, as Snogg-Sniffler scouts do, the secret instructions were sent out. "We is wanting the rest of the nifty-fifty now!" he bellowed. "When you does all get here, we does storm the embankment!"

The stomping of hooves scampered forwards.

Gurgling gasps for air puffed in and out.

Then out came the niftiest of all the Snogg-Snifflers in the King's army.

With battle cries, they charged onwards.

The scout and the It brothers, plus Granddad Sprinkle-Tinkle, were swept along.

"Put me down," panicked the old man. "I've never had a fair fight in me life."

"Is you always fiddling it?" asked a porker.

"Kind of … maybe … actually, yes," rattled the bag of old bones as they charged on.

The grassland, with its scattering of wild weeds, soon turned into trodden clumps. As they neared the pits covered in camouflage, mashed-in pasture became muddy land.

"You is doing proper work now!" cried a charging Snogg-Sniffler to the old man.

"You is not worry your brainy head!" yelled a speeding hog. "I is whipping through their defences faster than a racing greyhound."

Under hooves, the ground changed.

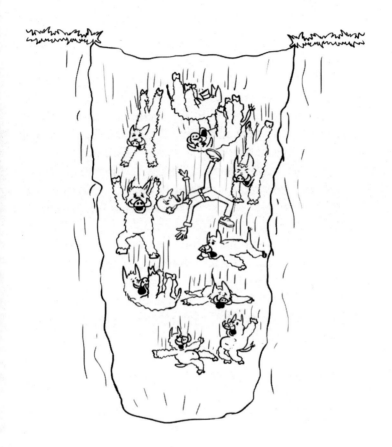

"We is having leg-springing movements now," declared the slowest of the nifty-fifty, as they bounced over the huge pit.

The deception worked. The covering gave way, and into the pit they all fell.

CHAPTER 18

IN THE HEAT OF WAR

While they squirmed in the bottom of the hole, the Snogg-Snifflers heard the giant ape shouting. "Wake up! Make for the fort!" cried Mr Tiggle-Trotter, hearing the struggling Snogg-Snifflers. "We're under attacked!" Then he grabbed hold of Frances, Mary and Godfrey. With striding limbs, he bounded over the terrain and jumped over the fortifications, calling to his origami army as he did so. "Call out the garrison! We are being attacked!" Now turning to check there had been no breaches in their defences, he cried, "To the parapets everyone … and make sure the ramparts are kept clear!"

Paper soldiers rushed out of the guardhouse and took position in the corner towers, flanking towers and all around the battlements.

It was only at that moment, after the giant ape had put them down, that Frances and Mary realised just how much had been done in such a short space of time by the paper army.

"Can you believe it?" gasped Frances Fidget-Knickers, in awe of the vast achievement.

The castle was massive, with covered parapets linking up with the towers. In defence, the turrets were manned and ready, as every available space was taken up by the origami army.

"This took one night to build?" gulped Mary in amazement.

In the inner circle were amassed a collection of wagons filled with military equipment.

"My word," smiled Godfrey in admiration. "You have been busy."

Mr Tiggle-Trotter hurried the clay officers along. "Up to the battlements with the water bombs."

The two girls and Godfrey hastily followed behind and were quickly at the top. "There's my grandfather," said Frances in disgust, as she looked over the edge.

"He's not very happy," laughed Mary, peering through the arrow loop.

With fingers curved, Granddad Sprinkle-Tinkle clawed at the sides of the walls. Overreacting with panic, he squawked, "How are we going to get out? Help! Do something! Anything! Just get me out of here!"

Godfrey climbed up onto the parapet. Sitting down on it, he stared down and chuckled. "Oh my, they're in a right pickle."

The pit was deep and the screams were loud.

"We is not earthworms burrowing through the dirt!" shouted a mud-covered hog.

"You is right," yelled a struggling Snogg-Sniffler. "We is food-grabbing, gobble-munching mercenaries, that's what we is!"

"When I is getting out," cried the commander, shaking a fist at anyone who was looking down, "my mood is shifting, and it be shifting your way!"

"I is agreeing," shouted the second in command. "The moment we is getting out you is all in for it!"

Up at the parapet, Frances asked, "Are we safe here? I mean, they can't get us up here, can they?"

Mary leant into the arrow loop and sniggered. "They can't even get out of a hole, let alone the mess they're making."

One second later, the water bombs pelted down.

First to throw them were the clay officers.

155

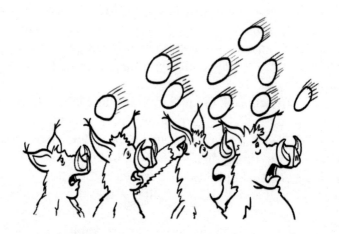

Then Godfrey.

Then the giant ape.

Then the origami army.

Finally, Frances and Mary let fly with their bombs filled with water.

"We is getting wet!" screamed a beast.

"It does get muddier!" yelped a hog.

The wriggling Snogg-Snifflers kept on churning up the mud.

Inspecting the commotion, the giant ape said, "If they start to work together as a team then they might stand a chance of getting out."

Arrows at the ready, the origami army drew their bows.

Mr Tiggle-Trotter gave the order to shoot. "Fire!"

A showering of paper arrows rained down, hitting their targets and bouncing straight back off the Snogg-Snifflers.

One of the beasts laughed. "They does have puny weapons. I has picked up a crumpled arrow. I does unwrap it. All this be fit for is cleaning myself after my do-doings."

Mary gasped. "Blimey, what are we going to do now? I mean, our weapons are useless – they didn't even make a mark, let alone a scratch."

"Miss Mary, you're forgetting Mr Tiggle-Trotter doesn't hurt any living thing."

"That's a lot of help in a war," insisted Mary, unimpressed. "Shall I just give up now and have done with it?"

Frances held out the box. "Mary, don't be silly – what about this?"

There was no time to answer, as Godfrey adjusted his monocle. Eye muscles clenching tight, he studied the situation. "Look – they're almost out!" he cried.

In the pit, bent-over Snogg-Snifflers made makeshift steps. Onto them the tallest Snogg-Snifflers stood, with their hooves digging into their fellow hogs' backs.

"You is doing good job," admired the commander.

A wincing boar moaned in pain. "They has not clipped their toes, Your Leadership. They is giving me terrible back pains."

The balancing beast grabbed hold of the very top edge of the pit and pulled. "You is shutting up and knuckling under or we is all stuck forever." With a yank and a kick, he was out. "Next one up, you is coming." He stretched out, leaning over to grab a hog.

Soon after that, they were all out –and not very happy.

Frances stared at the gap between them and the mud-covered brutes. "Seems like they've given up?"

"Miss Frances, never underestimate a Snogg-Sniffler … they hardly ever give in."

Suddenly, one of the beasts turned and threw a spear. Whistling with the force of the throw, it hit the castle wall. It plunged deep into the structure, with its tip pointing out the other side, leaving only a small piece sticking out on the side where it had gone in.

"Did you see that?" exclaimed Mary. "That's a javelin throw and a half!"

Instinctively, the giant ape sensed danger, as he shuddered, "They're doing something. I'm not sure what it is, but they're up to something, that's for sure."

CHAPTER 19

INTELLIGENCE-GATHERING

On the opposite side of the pit, his majesty was encouraged to come forwards. "You is okay to be coming out now – they has insignificant weapons! They is the puniest I has ever seen!"

From behind the castle walls, Frances and her friends saw one thousand Snogg-Snifflers move forwards, led by their monarch.

"Oh my," declared Godfrey, "there's the King of the Snogg-Snifflers. He's a lunatic of a brute. When I was a pup, he ransacked our village and took almost every rat and most of us pinkies." The image of being thrown down the latrine shook Godfrey. "If it wasn't for my mother and father hiding all of us in the excrement to disguise our scent, we'd have been caught as well."

Frances and Mary just listened, looking out over the approaching army of Snogg-Snifflers.

"They are savages, and the King is the worst of the lot," said the giant ape. "But all living things have a right to live their lives."

The army of hogs stopped just before the pit that surrounded the castle.

The King sniffed.

At the scent, he smiled, and then he bellowed to his troops, "I is smelling scaredy-cats!"

With glee, the commander stated, "They is reeking of their unpleasant emotions. If you is seeing, we has tested castle wall with spear. They has weak and paltry defences. But we is having troubles getting across to smash down castle wall. We does need bridging and breaching hogs."

"Bridging officer!" boomed the King.

"Breaching officer!" roared the royal hog.

And the monarch then bellowed again. "You is both coming here, quick fast!"

Back at the castle wall, all four continued their eagle-eyed surveillance.

"There's a lot of commotion going on over there," muttered Mary. "What do you think they're up to now?"

Frances looked at the box. It did not move.

"I don't think we're in immediate danger, or this would be shaking."

Godfrey reassured them both. "For the moment, Miss Frances and Miss Mary, we appear to be safe."

Using his lip-reading abilities to spy, the giant ape told them, "In the heat of battle, things can change very quickly. The King has asked for a couple of officers capable of breaking through our stronghold."

Mary wiggled a finger in her ear, as she went on to ask her question. "I didn't hear a thing – how did you know that?"

"I read lips," he answered.

Mary was about to ask some more but Frances came in. "When normal sound is not heard, you can understand speech by visually working out the movement of lips, face and tongue."

"You can do that?" asked Mary.

"Miss Mary, why don't we let Mr Tiggle-Trotter concentrate," said Godfrey, giving his attention to the giant ape. "Would you mind giving us an update?"

Fully focused, the great ape used his speech-reading abilities to repeat the information. "I, the King, is wanting bridging officer and breaching officer here right now. I has now asked twice. I is not asking three times as you is all knowing what happens when I is asking a third time."

Frances and Mary listened intently.

"The commander is talking now," spoke Mr Tiggle-Trotter, then repeating the words being spoken. "You is three strikes and we is off-chopping one of your legs. Hurry up or you is going home a bit lighter than you is coming here."

The giant ape stopped. Then he shuffled from right to left. Now searching with those enormous eyes, he went on. "Two Snogg-Snifflers are pushing their way to the King. It's looking like they have found the bridging and breaching officers. Let's see what they have to say."

Now the giant ape told it like a story.

"We is champions at three-legged race," proclaimed the bridging officer proudly.

"If we is losing a leg each," added the breaching officer, "we is not winning any more races for Your Majesty."

With a thoughtful sniff, the King snorted, "If you is not fixing problem, then I is chopping both your legs off and you is wiggling home like caterpillars."

Both officers swallowed hard.

Both officers' thoughts turned to the problem-solving.

Then they both put their best plans forwards.

161

First to go was the bridging officer. "Okay you is, Your High-Born One. I is needing to fill in hole and we is walking across."

"Sounds complicated," breathed the King.

As fast as a wink, the breaching officer replied, "When he is finished with very troublesome pit-filling, we does throw more spears into castle wall and we is all climbing up them like stairs."

Doubts washed over the King as he asked, "I is wanting to know how is you doing this filling of the pit?"

The bridging officer parted the army and ran up and down, with his plan of work coming out in between breaths. "We is digging whopping big hole behind our Snifflers here. Then the dirt we does take out of it, we does throw in this big hole in front of our army over there. When hole is all filled up, we does walk across, and then it's over to breaching officer because here and there has all been done."

The Snogg-Sniffler in charge of breaching barriers went on. "I is then getting Sniffler troops to throw loads of spears into castle wall and we is climbing up and breaking through their defences."

"I is sceptical with my reservations, so you is getting straight onto it," commanded the King, as a hive of activity took over.

Mr Tiggle-Trotter jolted out of his lip-reading activities and said, "They're going to make a fight of it after all."

Frances looked again at the box, and again it did not move. "What's wrong with it?" she worried.

With a nervous glance, Mary stuttered in a trembling voice, "P-P-Perhaps we've used up all of the magic Mrs Give-Us-A-Giggle's given us."

Stressing at every word, Godfrey sighed, "Without the box and its spellbinding powers, there's no way we can win if they breach these walls!"

Preparing to speak, the giant ape cleared his throat. "The origami army will put up a valiant fight. They will give us enough time to make a retreat if needs be."

"What about the farms?" asked Frances. "And all the people and their animals?"

There was no answer; only silence greeted their ears. It was as though an unspoken agreement had been made. Only the undertones of the Snogg-Snifflers broke them free from their stillness.

The King bellowed out, "Once we is over obstacles, we is not negotiating! Faster with your digging you is going! Faster with your filling I is wanting!"

Scampering around, the Snogg-Sniffler struggling under the pressure of his workload spluttered back, "I is doing as much as I is doing, and as fast as my hands is going, Your Majesty!"

"You is wise-cracking?" asked the royal one.

The mud-covered hog stopped.

He brushed himself clean.

Then he presented his argument to his sovereign.

"I does not crack wisely, Your Majesty," he insisted. "Instead, I is back-breaking and muddy with sweaty armpits – why is I the only one digging? If you does command more Snifflers to help, then we is getting it all done quicker than faster!"

The King gasped, for the argument was truly impressive. "That's even faster than quick." Then he pointed and ordered, "You is all up for dirt-digging as I is smelling relation. It be a scent relation to Him. Where is Him?"

All this time, Granddad Sprinkle-Tinkle had kept out of the way. He had stayed out of sight so as not to get volunteered for any more dangerous tasks.

In the background, a group of Snogg-Snifflers started with the earth-moving.

Instinctively, the other boars raised their snouts and sniffed for the old man. "We has smelt Him out!" cried a beast.

"You does having good sniffing," smiled the King.

"Does you want Him all hunky-dory, Your Majesty? Or does you want me to rattle and roll Him your way?" asked a porker.

"I is wanting Him here immediately," replied the King.

"Hokey-cokey, Your Majesty – rattling and rolling it does be!" cried the beast.

From the first shove, Granddad Sprinkle-Tinkle was rattled through the ranks like a pinball. "What's going on? Is this any way to treat an old man?" he yelped.

A hog lifted him up.

The old man complained bitterly. "I have you know, without me brains intact, you'll be getting no ideas!" he moaned, just before he was thrown to another brute.

"You is not worrying your brainy head," laughed the catching Snogg-Sniffler. "I has safe hands, unlike Sniffler over there."

Up into the air Granddad Sprinkle-Tinkle went, as the nasty old bag of bones cried out, "Help! Don't you drop me!"

Down he came and was caught by a jesting hog. "If I is dropping you, I is catching you again, only after you has done a dead-cat bounce."

Then Granddad Sprinkle-Tinkle was stood up and belly-shoved, which propelled him in front of the King. "There you is," smiled the monarch. "I is smelling family relations. I is wondering, has you sneaked anyone back?"

The old man straightened himself and answered shakily, "Why would I want to do that? It would mean sharing."

"Good," sniffed the King, "as I is sniffing humans up there. It is only little smelling, and it be having a brief, faint smell, just like you is whiffing."

Granddad Sprinkle-Tinkle took a gander at the castle. Inspecting it more closely, he caught a glimpse of Frances, just as she ducked out of sight.

With wretched contempt, he blasted, "There's no way I'm letting you off the hook this time, girly! A leech, that's what you are – sucking all the attention away from me! This time you will be removed from my sight forever, and sold into slavery!"

As Frances sank to her knees, she breathed deeply, feeling her body pounding with nervousness. "Whatever have I done to upset my grandfather so?"

Godfrey sighed. "Jealousy is a strong and powerful emotion, Miss Frances. Everything was fine until you were born. You mother, rightly so, turned her attention from her father to you."

Mary crawled under the parapet and comforted her friend. "Don't you listen to him – he's just a selfish and greedy old so and so. He's only interested in himself. Out for number one alone – why should we bother taking him home?"

Mr Tiggle-Trotter sighed. "You are under orders from Judge Get-It-Wrong. Sometimes in life, we have to do things we don't like to do. For you two, this is one of those times."

Frances felt a swelling of determination brewing inside her body as the nerves faded away. Pulling her friend to her feet, she said, "I'm pretty sure we are not finished with this box just yet. Mrs Give-Us-A-Giggle would never let us down. I hope when we are in need, my grandfather gets his comeuppance!"

Godfrey, with a sense of admiration, comforted Frances Fidget-Knickers. "That's the spirit, Miss Frances. Never say never, as they say. And they say also, it's not over until the fat lady sings … although I'm not sure what that one means."

"It means," frowned Frances, regaining her mental attitude of a thirst for knowledge, "it's not over till it's over and done with. You know – don't count your chickens before they hatch." She stood her ground and insisted, "If a fight is what they want, then our origami army will give them one."

CHAPTER 20

THE BATTLE ENDS

As hundreds of Snogg-Snifflers sprinted back and forth with their earth-moving movements, the hole was beginning to fill.

Unfortunately, the King was not a patient ruler.

"Hurrying up," instructed the King, "or I is hoof-kicking your backsides. All this waiting around is being a nightmare. Where be my in-betweeners?"

"Is you meaning Pick-it, Roll-It and Flick-It, Your Majesty?" asked the commander.

"I is, and you is finding them."

The order was passed down from the commander to the second in command. "The King does want the in-betweeners."

The second in command passed on the information to the next hog in line. Head after head turned from side to side, relaying the information until it got to the It brothers.

"The King is wanting a tin-built steamer," declared a beast, passing on the mixed-up information.

"That be a coded message," sniffed Pick-It, trying to sniff up some snot.

"We is needing to work it out," gazed Roll-It, eagerly watching his brother's snot gurgle.

"I has already done so," stated Flick-It. "We is the in-betweeners and the King is wanting us." Then he said to the nearest unrelated hog, "Tell the King we is coming."

Again, the heads turned from side to side, relaying the message until it got to the commander, and he repeated the message to his royal highness. "Tell the King we is humming."

168

His majesty smiled. "You is never being too careful with secret messaging. When they is turning up, at least I is hearing them."

All at once, the sky darkened as it was filled with a volley of origami arrows.

For protection, the monarch took cover. Bodyguards, with no knowledge of the paper arrows, bundled on top of his royal highness.

He got squashed.

Now under a pile of porkers, the King flinched. "It be a little uncomfortable under here … is I safe?"

The projectiles bounced off the commander, as he laughed, "You is not worrying about their futile attempts to be making war. See – they has useless weapons."

The King winced under the weight of the several beasts that were squashing him. "Is you sure I is safe to come out?"

"You is perfectly safe, and I is showing you," chuckled the commander, picking up an arrow and thrusting it at the King's snout.

The paper arrow crumpled on impact. "I has tough skin," stated the monarch. "I does not need protection anymore – off you is getting now."

As the royal one got up, Pick-It, Roll-It and Flick-It presented themselves to their sovereign.

"Our Overlord, I be Pick-It," beamed one hog, holding up a pointed finger with a huge bogey on the end of it. "Look, see – I has my nose working again."

"Our Crown-Headed One, I be Roll-It," said another hog, taking the snot from his brother. With a goofy grin, he declared, "Look, see – my hands is all getting soft again with rolling it."

"Our Sultan of Excellence, I is Flick-It," informed the last of the brothers, taking the ready-made pellet of mucus. "I is showing you my skillfulness."

He fired it.

It shot through the air, hitting the end of the spear sticking out of the castle wall. "Look, see – I is never missing."

With a mighty big smile, the King expressed his admiration. "You does all have skills."

"We does," they all answered.

"I has been informed you is all skilled in catapulting," said the emperor of all the Snogg-Snifflers. "It be a new technology our engineering officer has invented. He is telling me you is experienced in flinging – is this being true?"

They all stood proudly with big smiles.

"We is flung up into the sky," beamed Pick-It.

"We is flying like birds while we is up there," grinned Roll-It.

"But we is not all delicate and breaking, like wing-flutters," insisted Flick-It.

With a snout-rubbing hand, the King ground his teeth. "We has no rocks here. We is testing castle walls, and you has all just volunteered for the job as my missiles. You three is all going to be our boulders, as I is not sure of spear working," he grunted.

A large machine with some new modifications was dragged forwards. The contraption had been improved from the one that was used in the canyon.

Mary was the first to spot it. "Whatever is that thing?" she asked.

"It appears to be a device of some sort, Miss Mary. I'm not quite sure what they're up to."

Mr Tiggle-Trotter shuddered. "Siege weapon," he trembled.

Frances scratched her head. "It seems a bit odd to have a giant catapult and no ammunition to use. If you look around, there's nothing but flat grassland stretching back to the horizon. What will they use for ammunition?"

"Wait a minute – they can't be, can they?" asked Mary. "They're using Snogg-Snifflers?"

Godfrey twitched rather nervously. "I told you the King was ruthless. He'll stop at nothing to get his own way."

The pit had now been filled in.

It formed a path between the warring boars and the fortress.

In a concerned voice, the giant ape said, "We were safe all the while we maintained the gap. Now there's no stopping them."

Next to the catapult, the King schemed over his plan. "Pick-It, you is first to go."

"Righty ho, I is, Your Majesty."

"After you has hit castle wall, you is getting up and running back as we is firing Roll-It over your head."

"Trotting back fast and quick I is, Your Majesty."

171

"After Roll-It is hitting castle wall, he is getting back up and running back as we is firing Flick-It over his head."

"He is doing it most splendidly, Your Majesty."

"When Flick-It is hitting castle wall, you, Pick-It, does be firing again."

"I is whacking it good and proper hard, Your Majesty."

The King smiled. "As you is seeing, I is kind to the environment by recycling my ammunition."

"You is considerate king, Your Majesty."

The monarch went on. "We is keeping with the bombardment until castle wall gives way. How is you liking my plan?"

"You has brilliant planning strategy, and we is ready to put it to a test, Your Evilness," declared all three.

Into the device went Pick-It, as the machine was inspected by the engineering officer. "You is rolling up into a tight ball now. That way you is making better smashing when you is bashing against castle defences," insisted the maker of mechanical contraptions.

"Ready!" bellowed the King.

"We is," answered the inventor of the machine.

"Steady!" boomed the King.

"We is," replied the maker of wonderments.

"Go!" hollered the King, giving his command.

"Right you is, Your Majesty," replied the engineering officer, pulling a lever.

Now rolled tight into a ball, Pick-It was catapulted up into the air. Hurtling towards the castle wall, he cried, "I does put my back into it!" With a smack, he hit the wall with a tremendous thud. The impact shook the structure, as the hog tumbled down. "See? I does whack it good and proper hard!" he declared.

Running back, he saw his brother Roll-It flying head first. With a smash, he head-butted the wall. "I is using my noddle!" he shouted.

Just as Pick-It got back to the catapult, the twanging noise of Flick-it sounded out. Speeding towards the castle, he stuck out his belly. "Splat" went the belly-flop. "I is tummy-bashing!" he cried.

Like a juggling act, the brothers kept going until some cracks appeared in the defences.

Inside the castle, the origami army tried to repair the crumbling fortress.

"It's no good!" cried Mr Tiggle-Trotter, as one of the brothers hit the wall again. "Any minute now they will have broken through!"

Still the bombing echoed out with each bang, crash, wallop of a whack.

Inside the castle, they could hear shouts of joy from the army on the other side.

"It's giving way!" shouted Godfrey, as large chunks started to fall.

With thud after thud, the opening became bigger.

Inside the castle, panic was starting to set in.

"We could sure use some help – is the box doing anything now?" asked Mary.

The box didn't move. "What's wrong with it?" worried Frances, watching the rest of the wall collapse.

"Defend the castle!" cried the giant ape, as clay officers instructed the origami army into battle.

"Make ready with your arrows!" cried Mr Tiggle-Trotter, giving his order.

Bows were stretched back and took aim, the projectiles with their pointed tips ready to fire.

"Godfrey, take Frances and Mary and fetch the mud you collected last night," instructed the giant primate. As they tried to ask why, he said, "No time to explain – now hurry with it, and don't forget the water."

Through the dust they heard the King of the Snogg-Snifflers rousing his troops. "Is I not telling you, they is weaklings!"

The marauding army of Snogg-Snifflers cheered their king with deafening war cries.

His royal highness bellowed over them, "I is telling you they is yellow bellies!"

With the waving of arms, more cheers cried out from the army of hogs. "You is, you is, you is!" came the replies.

Still the King fuelled the speech with contempt, and boomed, "We is exploiting weakness and crushing cowardly custards!"

Ear-shattering battle cries blasted out. "We does, we does, we does!" they shrieked.

The royal hog waved over his army and thundered. "Is you ready to make mincemeat of them?"

In a frenzy of excitement, the Snogg-Sniffler army sniffed and snorted. "We is, we is, we is!" came their answers.

Then only one word came bellowing out from the royal mouth. "Charge!"

Bursting forth with battling screams, the castle defenders were greeted with insults.

"You is cluck, cluck like chickens," screamed a charging Snogg-Sniffler, "and we is cracking open your heads like eggs!"

"I is smelling rat," screeched a clambering hog. "Come to hoggy and I is pulling out your insides!"

"Humans!" cried out a blockheaded Snogg-Sniffler. "I is peeling off your skin and making nice bag for my wife!"

Inside the castle, the giant ape said, "Don't take any notice of them; they are only trying to scare you."

"Really?" exclaimed Mary Midget-Mouth, shuddering at the thought of being peeled like an apple. "They're doing a very good job of it."

"Fire!" shouted Mr Tiggle-Trotter, as a hail of arrows shot out. Then he gave the order, "Fire at will!"

Now scrambling over the rubble, the Snogg-Snifflers were hit with a showering of slender darts.

Most of them bounced off.

Some of them got stuck in awkward places.

"I is having clean ears," snorted a hog, disgusted, pulling out a paper shaft. On the end of it was a lump of dark brown earwax. "I has only washed them out two years ago."

A beast who looked like he had chopsticks stuck up both nostrils bitterly complained. "They is trying to suffocate me!" With a nose sneeze, they were expelled. "They has worthless weaponry," he snorted.

Opening his mouth wide to scream, a few paper arrows went inside and down one hog's throat. He coughed and spat out the straight sticks. "I has had my tonsils out ages ago, and if that is all you has got, I is ripping out yours and skewering them to make tonsil kebabs."

With their orders given, the clay officers led the origami army and clashed with the invaders. Great crushing blows were simply shrugged off by the Snogg-Snifflers.

Paper men were torn to shreds in the conflict.

Injured clay officers with missing limbs made their way back for medical treatment.

"Godfrey," cried the giant ape, "hurry – we need to mend them!"

"Right you are," answered the rat. "Now, Miss Frances, you will be making legs and feet, and Miss Mary, you will be making arms and hands. Over here, I will be patching the clay officers up so we can send them back to the frontline."

A medical line for corrective therapy with artificial limbs churned out the body parts. The workload made the two girls a little breathless.

"Here you go, Godfrey," puffed Frances.

There was no time for the formal tone of the rat, as he worked tirelessly repairing the clay people. "Can I have some arms and hands next?" he asked.

"Here they are," panted Mary, rushing over with her pile of sculpted body parts.

Godfrey worked away as stumps were turned into fully working limbs again. As one clay patient was made better, the next one stood uncomplaining with its dreadful injuries. Godfrey took a deep breath. Rushing from one officer to the next, he quickly returned then to duty.

The giant primate cried in anguish, "We're giving it all we've got! It looks like we are fighting a losing battle! We can't hold them back for much longer!"

Then out of the blue, the box started to shake.

It was a tiny little shake.

The tiny little shake was so small that Frances almost missed it. "Oh my," she gasped, as a fluffy ball of brown fur appeared, no bigger than a loaf of bread.

The whatever-it-was opened its eyes; it looked cuter than a little kitten.

Mary looked unimpressed and joked, "What's it going to do – snuggle them to death?"

"No," came a voice from the box as they heard Mrs Give-Us-A-Giggle explain. "It's a Fang-Snapper, me dears. It does look kind of adorable, don't you think? Now don't let that fool you, though, because that's how they lure in their prey. Fang-Snappers have very potent bites. Their venom can make you do all sorts of silly things. Just remember to give your instruction." The message started to fade as they heard the white witch talking to one of her customers. "Bye, me dears … now where was I, Mrs Gabble-Gob…?"

"At least someone is getting the right attention," Mary cringed, as the Snogg-Snifflers overpowered the origami army.

With great unease, Godfrey stressed, "Miss Frances, now would be a good time to give your orders!"

"Would you mind," began Frances Fidget-Knickers, starting to ask the Fang-Snapper for assistance, "as you can see we're in a right pickle, could you help us, please?"

The Fang-Snapper yawned and did nothing.

Brushing himself clean from the mud, Godfrey stressed, "Miss Frances, don't forget to point, as you need to give them direction!"

Frances Fidget-Knickers did just that with an outstretched finger. "Snogg-Snifflers only, thank you very much."

A sea of brown fur rattled out of the box.

The King spotted this sea of brown fur heading his way. "Look, you is seeing!" he cried to Granddad Sprinkle-Tinkle. "They has brought appetisers!"

With a yank, the old man was heading into battle.

Trying to deflect from his cowardice, he spluttered, "It's not safe for you in there, Your Majesty. Your Royal Highness might get hurt or even killed!"

"Me is thinking," began the King, "your problem is you is being too nice. You is needing to stop with your sissy ways. A bit of battling is changing all that nicely-nicely in you."

Now entering the thick of it, the devious old man got an elbow in the face.

"Whack" went the blow. "Ouch," he gasped, dropping to the floor.

"You is not staying there," laughed the monarch. "We has fighting to do."

More accidental power-shots hit Granddad Sprinkle-Tinkle. "Ouch, ouch, ouch!" he spluttered after each thump.

The King weaved and bobbed in and out of the punches without getting hit. "You is needing to learn ducking and diving … it all be in the footwork," he smiled.

Punch-drunk and wobbling, the old man slurred, "I was never any good at dancing as I always had two left feet."

"You is not having a little worry – in a minute I is getting you a right foot," snorted the King as the Fang-Snappers started to attack.

With deadly speed, the swarming balls of fur darted in and out, sinking their fangs into the battling hogs.

"I is being bitten like fleas," yelped a scratching boar.

The Fang-Snappers kept biting.

"They has an infestation," moaned a beast.

With insect abilities, the bites irritated their skin as the poison was absorbed.

Frances, Mary and Godfrey, along with the giant ape, watched as the effects of the toxins took over.

"My legs has stopped working!" panicked a porker as his face dropped.

"I has floppy arms!" cried a Sniffler, as his eyelids filled up with water.

179

Crying uncontrollably, a beast sobbed, "I is knowing what you is meaning, as I is drowning in my own tears!"

At the sight of the Snogg-Sniffler army falling like skittles, Granddad Sprinkle-Tinkle cried, "What's happening?"

The King answered, as the onslaught continued, "I is infuriated – they is using biological warring tricks!"

"Are they?" asked the old man.

"We is battling on treacherous ground," snarled the monarch.

"Are we?" gabbled the coward of all grandfathers. "Don't you think it's time we were leaving? After all, I still have a treasure to spend."

Around them, the Snogg-Sniffler army was being picked off in huge quantities.

Their majesty growled, "We is standing in the face of annihilation, and all you is thinking of is your own skin!"

Now was the time to show the blister's true colours; rattling on, the horrid old gutless weasel ran away. "Get lost – you're a loser, and I'm second best to no one," he spat.

"I is knuckle-dusting you when we is meeting next!" cried the King. Then all at once a Fang-Snapper bit him. As the toxic liquid spread through his body, he mellowed into dreamy time. "They has the most potent of magic. Does you like my hat?" he smiled soppily.

The old man bumped into a couple of infected boars.

"Take my hands," spoke one hog in a dazed and dreamlike state. "I think my legs is sinking."

With arms outstretched, the beast next to him screamed, "I has no hands, my eyes has stopped seeing!"

From a distance, Frances could see her horrid relative trying to escape. "Oh yes," she said to the Fang-Snappers. "Can you stop my grandfather? But no biting."

180

Tiny squeals were made as the furry foes blocked off the horrid old man's escape.

Legs slightly apart, Granddad Sprinkle-Tinkle was surrounded by a snarling bunch of Fang-Snappers. Talking with clicks and whistles, they made their plans.

"I'm done for – never to spend a penny of me booty," he whimpered.

The parting of his legs presented the perfect opportunity as a ball of fur darted forwards. The soft dangly collection of boy bits got hit.

"ME NUTS!" cried the old man as he doubled over. Cupping his private parts, he winced through clenched teeth. "It hurts!" Rolling over and curling up, he coughed out, "You've crushed me whatsits!" Coughing and spluttering with pained gasps, he wheezed, "I'm not sure if I will ever pee the same again!"

Mary Midget-Mouth jumped for joy. "Right in the middle wicket, as my father would say."

"My," cringed Godfrey, "that does look painful."

The giant ape flinched. "What goes around comes around."

With an uncaring glance, Frances Fidget-Knickers frowned. "You can bite him now – after what he's put us through, it's the least he deserves."

Needle-sharp teeth gripped Granddad Sprinkle-Tinkle's leg. "They're eating me alive!" he cried out. Then the mind-altering venom took effect. "Do you want vegetables with it? I recommend you roast both of them first."

After that, he passed out, while the Snogg-Sniffler army lay all around, mumbling mumbo-jumbo.

Godfrey quickly reminded the two girls, "Quick, Miss Frances and Miss Mary – now's your chance to rescue him."

Unexpectedly, the box did something strange as they reached the old man.

It shook uncontrollably.

Frances let it go.

The wooden container fell apart and reconstructed itself.

In front of them now was a door.

It opened.

Standing inside was Mrs Give-Us-A-Giggle. "Hello, me dears," she beamed, waving them forwards.

Mr Tiggle-Trotter smiled. "Looks like you are going home. At least you didn't get hung, drawn and quartered."

Godfrey shuddered. "Nasty business, being strung up and then them drawing pictures of you," he tutted.

"It certainly is," agreed the giant ape. "Only for them to cut the artwork into four pieces."

Mary just stood there, her mouth open in disbelief, as her friend smiled and said, "I should have known that not all things are the same in this world."

Godfrey helped them push Granddad Sprinkle-Tinkle through the open door. "I'll be staying behind, Miss Frances, and helping Mr Tiggle-Trotter clear up this mess."

"Now, me dears," smiled Mrs Give-Us-A-Giggle, "I'll just get time back to where it was before it all started. By the way, I wish I could be there when this sorry sight of a grandfather wakes up."

Goodbyes were said and before they knew it, Mary, Frances and the old man were back in the cottage at the exact spot Granddad Sprinkle-Tinkle last stood before his abduction.

With their stories ready, Frances and Mary waited for him to wake up.

"Get them off me!" shouted the worst grandparent ever. "Stop biting me!" he cried, jiggling his body.

"Granddad," said Frances, pretending to show concern, "are you alright?"

"Where am I?" he asked dizzily, as the room went spinning around him.

"You're at home," answered Mary. "I heard you fall so we ran in to see if you were okay."

Regaining the attitude of a nasty stink-bomb, he moaned, "Okay, she said! Are you alright, she asked! Do I look and feel okay is what I say! No, of course I don't!"

With the very last drop of venom suddenly taking hold, he turned and said nicely, "I'm off to me room for a rest. Why don't you take the rest of the day off?"

So that's what they did until the next time Godfrey caught up with them – and what an adventure that was going to turn out to be.

FRANCES FIDGET-KNICKERS

AND THE CHANCE TO GET EVEN

Colin Wicks

The hilariously funny first book by Colin Wicks.
Available from Amazon as a paperback, or eBook.

Spot the difference

Just for fun, there are six things different with these pictures, can you find them all.